I0648384

Anonymous

For Things you Ought to Know Inquire Within

where you will find valuable and useful information, and a reliable

shopping guide

Anonymous

For Things you Ought to Know Inquire Within
where you will find valuable and useful information, and a reliable shopping guide

ISBN/EAN: 9783337082086

Printed in Europe, USA, Canada, Australia, Japan

Cover: Foto ©Andreas Hilbeck / pixelio.de

More available books at **www.hansebooks.com**

FOR

Things You Ought to Know

INQUIRE WITHIN,

WHERE YOU WILL FIND

Valuable ⚭ Useful Information,

AND A RELIABLE

Shopping Guide.

PHILADELPHIA:
BURK & McFETRIDGE,
Publishers and Printers,
Nos. 306-308 Chestnut Street.

COPYRIGHT, 1885, BY

BURK & McFETRIDGE,

PHILADELPHIA, **PA.**

Press of Burk & McFetridge.
306-308 Chestnut St.

A COMPLETE GUIDE

TO

Atlantic City

CONTAINING,

*Among other Useful Information, a List of Hotels,
their Capacity and Rates, and
Leading Stores,*

WITH

SHOPPING GUIDE.

HOTEL GUIDE.

HOTELS	NO. OF SLEEPING ROOMS	RATE PER DAY		PER WEEK		SEE PAGE
Albion	163	3 50		....		....
Aldine	22	2 00		8 00	12 00	36
Acme	26	2 00		8 00	15 00	....
Argyle	35	2 00	2 50	10 00	15 00	....
Ashland	85	2 50		8 00	15 00	35
Arlington	25	2 00		9 00	15 00	....
Atglen	30	1 50	2 00	8 00	10 00	....
Brighton	125	4 00	5 00		25 00	....
Berkeley	50	3 00		15 00	20 00	....
Bellevue	31	2 00	2 50	10 00	15 00	....
Bedloe's	50	2 00		10 00	12 00	....
Bailey	12	2 00		10 00	15 00	....
Colonnade	65	3 00		18 00	20 00	26
Chester County House	80	2 00	2 75		12 50	34
Clarendon	35	3 00		12 00	16 00	32
Chalfonte	80	3 00		15 00	20 00	34
Champion	16	2 00			12 00	....
Chatham	18	2 00		10 00	12 00	....
Central House	48	2 00		12 00	18 00	....
Clifton	39	2 00		8 00	12 00	....
Continental	19	2 00		8 00	12 00	36
Dennis	113	3 00	4 00	18 00	30 00	....
Dudley Arms	40	2 50		12 00	15 00	36
Elberon	40	2 50	3 00	15 00	20 00	34
Edgewater	24	2 00	2 50	10 00	15 00	29
Emerson	63	2 00	2 50	12 00	15 00	34
Florida	35	3 00		12 00	18 00	....
Haddon	60	3 00		16 00	20 00	31
Hygeia	22	2 00	2 50	12 00	15 00	36
Heeklers	28	2 00		10 00	12 00	....
Jackson House	35	3 00	3 50	15 00	18 00	....
Kentucky House	33	2 50		12 00	18 00	....
Kuehnie's	50	2 00	2 50	12 00	16 00	....
Lancaster	18	2 00	2 50	10 00	15 00	36
Lansdale	33	2 00	2 50	10 00	12 00	36
Leeds' Cottage	40	1 50	2 00	8 00	12 00	36
Lynn	20	2 00		12 00	15 00	....
Liddlesdale	12	2 00	2 50	10 00	15 00	....

HOTEL GUIDE.

HOTELS — CONTINUED	NO. OF SLEEPING ROOMS	RATE PER DAY		PER WEEK		SEE PAGE
Le Pierre's	20	2 50		15 00		....
Margate	51	3 00		15 00	18 00	27
Mansion	200	3 00		18 00	21 00	....
Mentone	20	1 50	3 00	10 00	15 00	....
Mercer House	50	....		4 00		....
Manhattan	24	2 00		10 00		....
Metropolitan	60	2 00		8 00	12 00	....
Merchants	40	2 50		12 00	15 00	....
Malatesta's	60	2 50	3 00	12 00	18 00	....
Ocean House	75	3 00		15 00	18 00	32
Ocean Villa	20	2 00		8 00	15 00	37
Penn Mansion	38	2 50		10 00	15 00	....
Royal	80					33
Ruscumbe	40	2 50		12 00	15 00	....
Radnor	15	1 50	2 00	9 00	12 00	37
Radcliff House	29	2 00		10 00	15 00	....
Revere	40	2 50		12 00	20 00	37
Renovo	24	2 00		10 00	12 00	37
Stockton	84	3 00		18 00		28
Sea Side	80	3 00		16 00	20 00	25
Seabright	35	3 00		15 00	20 00	....
Senate House	60	3 00		15 00		....
Stafford	32	2 50	3 00	10 00	18 00	....
Shelburne	75	....				....
St. Charles	100	2 50		10 00	18 00	....
Schaufler's	150	2 50		16 00		....
Traymore	117	3 00	5 00	18 00	25 00	....
Tremont	48	2 50	3 00	10 00	14 00	....
United States	250	3 00	3 50	18 00	25 00	30
Victoria	60	2 00	2 50	10 00	12 00	....
Vermont	35	2 00	2 50	12 00	18 00	....
Waverley	85	3 00		16 00	25 00	....
Wilton	16	2 50		10 00	15 00	....
Wellington	43	2 00	2 50	10 00	15 00	....
Westminster	35	2 00		10 00	12 00	36
Windsor	56	2 50	3 00	18 00	20 00	....
Willard	21	2 00	2 50	12 00	15 00	....
Wetherill	24	2 00		10 00	15 00	35

THOMAS HOLT,
City Stove Works

FARMERS' BOILERS,

CASTINGS
AND
HOLLOW-WARE.

Oil and Gasoline Stoves
and Trimmings.

STOVES,

HEATERS,

RANGES
AND
REPAIRS.

111 and 113 North Second Street,   PHILADELPHIA.

Agent for { CHARLES NOBLE & CO., Philadelphia.
RATHBONE, SARD & CO., Albany, N. Y.
FULLER-WARREN CO., Troy, N. Y.

Leading Stores in Atlantic City.

CONTENTS.

Beautify Your Homes

WITH

"PATENTED"

Stained Glass SUBSTITUTE

It produces all the effects of the genuine glass that costs from

10 to 30 times the Price.

It can be easily applied to old or new glass without removing the sash.

Samples by Mail, 25 Cents.

Send for Illustrated Catalogue and Price-List.

W. C. YOUNG, Sole Agent,

731 Arch Street, - Philadelphia.

J. C. WAHL,

A Complete Assortment of

Fine Shoes

Cor. Atlantic and Virginia Avenues.

THE LEADING

Dry Goods House

OF ATLANTIC CITY

Nos. 1619 and 1621 Atlantic Avenue,

Branch of N. W. Cor. 9th & Washington Ave., Philada.

UNDERWEAR.

Ladies', Gents' and Children's Summer and Winter Goods always on hand.

Dress Cloths and Cassimeres at Lowest Cash Prices.

All leading makes of Muslins at Lowest Prices. Table Linens, Napkins, Towels, Notions, and Toilet Articles.

We extend a cordial invitation to the ladies of this city and the surrounding country.   Yours respectfully,

THOMPSON IRVIN.

Prescription Family Medicine Store

GALBREATH, APOTHECARY,

PACIFIC AVENUE, COR. NEW YORK,

ATLANTIC CITY, N. J.

The store is connected by Telephone with all prominent Hotels, and other places on the Island, also with Philadelphia and other prominent Cities. Articles of any kind not on hand will be ordered from City and delivered in the shortest possible time.

Messenger boys on hand at all hours. Orders from Hotels sent for and delivered promptly.

We request a visit to our handsome and thoroughly furnished establishment.

ATLANTIC CITY, N. J.

This gay city, so popular among all classes of society, has not only obtained its fame as a summer resort, but is also a great seaside city, where in every part of the year health and pleasure-seekers crowd the hotels and its famous beach. In summer the magnificent bathing, fishing and sailing attract thousands, whilst its popularity as a summer resort is almost equaled by its fame as a winter retreat. It seems to have been marked out by nature where all the forces needed for the constitution are centralized. The beach is fine; the surf-bathing famous; the fishing and sailing superb. It is supplied with every convenience that can contribute to the health and comfort of its inhabitants. The sewerage system is good, and the water is from fresh springs of the mainland, and is both pure and wholesome. There are many very handsome hotels and pretty cottages, which lend attraction to all comers.

The whole of the buildings in Atlantic City are built entirely of wood with one or two exceptions, from the largest hotel with its tall towers to the smallest cottage or store, and in several styles of archi-

COST OF LIVING IN ATLANTIC CITY.

Seaside resorts are usually expensive places at which to live, and Atlantic City was at one time no exception to this rule. During the last two years, however, a decided change has taken place, and to-day Atlantic City is the cheapest summer resort in the United States.

This is due, no doubt, to the indefatigable efforts of a firm known as Finley Acker & Co. This enterprising firm has a large Coffee Roasting and Tea Establishment at 123 North Eighth Street, Philadelphia, and a Wholesale Grocery at 132 Market Street. To accommodate their numerous patrons who summer at Atlantic, they opened a branch house there about two years ago, and sold their goods at exactly the same prices as in their Philadelphia stores. Their Coffees and Teas had long before gained an extensive reputation for superiority, and it was not long before Atlantic City residents took advantage of their superior goods. Their coffee trade grew to such a magnitude that they contemplated roasting their coffees in Atlantic City; but as it would have been impracticable to put in the elaborate machinery used in their Roasting Establishment in Philadelphia, they secured much better results by roasting it daily and shipping it down while warm, in airtight cans. At the earnest request of their patrons they gradually added to their stock until now it embraces everything in the fine and fancy grocery line including the finest creamery butter and imported fruits and nuts. They have greatly enlarged their store (which by the way, is at 922 Atlantic Avenue, between Maryland and Virginia), and if you call on them you will not only find them obliging and courteous but will very likely save considerable money during the season. They offer a complete price list to each customer, so that their patrons know the exact cost of every article.

A. L. HELMBOLD'S

JELLY OF GLYCERINE AND ROSES

FOR SUNBURN AND MOSQUITO BITES.

Endorsed by ADELINA PATTI, FANNY DAVENPORT, ADELAIDE RISTORI, and others.

HELMBOLD'S
JELLY OF GLYCERINE AND ROSES.
For Rendering the SKIN SOFT and SMOOTH, and Al-
laying Smarting caused by SUNBURN, and ROUGHNESS result-
ing from COLD WINDS and IMPURE SOAPS.
DIRECTIONS—Apply the Jelly immediately after washing, before the SKIN is dry.

A. L. HELMBOLD'S
TEMPLE OF PHARMACY,
CONTINENTAL HOTEL, PHILADELPHIA.
25c.   OPEN ALL NIGHT   25c.

Originally Prepared 1882.   **PRICE, 25 CENTS.**

A PREPARATION FOR ALL

It never disappoints always pleases.
You want it for *Chapped Hands Chapped
Lips, Sunburn, Freckles, Chafing*,
And all roughness of the skin caused by
impure soaps, etc.

Originated and Prepared only by
A. L. Helmbold, Temple of Pharmacy,
CONTINENTAL HOTEL,
830 Chestnut St., Philadelphia.

Sold by all Druggists.   Trade Mark Registered.

DAVID JOHNSTON'S

Bottling ✦ Establishment

OFFICE, LANSDALE HOUSE,

NORTH CAROLINA AVE.   ATLANTIC CITY, N. J.

Mineral Waters, Sarsaparilla, Ginger Ale, Porter, Ale, Lager and Weiss
Beer, Brown Stout Porter, Seltzer, Appollinaris Water.

ORDERS PROMPTLY ATTENDED TO.

tecture, thus affording the house painter ample scope to display his abilities by applying the colors to suit the style of building; this has been done in many cases in a very artistic manner by using the Ajax paint, manufactured by Howell & Co., of Race Street, Philadelphia, of which O. H. Guttridge, of 1003 Atlantic Avenue is the Agent. The United States Hotel has been newly painted with this paint, which not only gives the building a very pleasing effect but preserves the wood against the action of the weather.

Atlantic City has no particular characteristics. It stands entirely by itself; as a seaside resort it combines all the advantages of other places without any of their extreme views. People can enjoy themselves according to their own inclinations, as long as they remain within bounds. It is like one seaside resort without its beer and rowdyism —like another without its religion; another without its temperance and cheapness, and another without its dissipation and extravagances. Here the extremely good come to be moderately bad, and the extremely bad to be moderately good, if they can. Pleasure no doubt does here reign supreme, still religion has not been forgotten, for every denomination has its place of worship. See pages 25 and 27.

F. A. LUDWIG

THE RELIABLE

PHILADELPHIA ✦ HOUSEFURNISHING ✦ STORE

CHINA AND QUEENSWARE, CLASS, MAJOLICA, EARTHEN, TIN, WOOD AND WILLOWWARE.

Cutlery and Silverware, Lamps and Lamp Goods a Speciality. All at Philadelphia Prices.

All Goods warranted as represented.

Estimates for Hotels and Cottages Cheerfully Given.

Nos. 1907 AND 1909 ATLANTIC AVENUE.

C. E. Ulmer, D. D. S.

(Surgeon Dentist.)

Gas Prepared Fresh Daily.

Night Calls Attended To.

Office, 1112 Atlantic Avenue,

(Next to Mansion House.)

SMALL PROFITS. — **QUICK SALES.**

THE CHEAPEST PLACE, THE BEST PLACE,

TO BUY

FURNITURE, CARPETS

OIL CLOTHS AND BEDDING,

AT THE

GRAND DEPOT,

ATLANTIC AVE., NEAR CITY HALL.

Upholstering in all its branches. Carpets, Matting, Oil Cloth, etc., Laid. Mattresses made and renovated. Veranda Awnings made to order. Furniture repaired and varnished.

The Upholstering Department will be under the able management of Mr. J. C. Hoffman, formerly of No. 1711 Atlantic avenue, and satisfaction is guaranteed.

The Atlantic City GRAND DEPOT is the largest and best stocked house furnishing establishment in this part of the country, without any exception.

BELL TELEPHONE No. 74. **OSCAR PEIKERT.**

Although the student of botany will find in Atlantic City a very limited field for his studies, still, if he turns his mind for the time being to the study of human nature he will find here plenty to do. He can scarcely make a mistake as to the time of year when he visits Atlantic City. If he likes crowds, let him choose the summer ; if he requires a quiet life, let him visit some other seaside resort, or come here in winter. There is nothing in life like success, and so it is with Atlantic City ; its success is certain, for, thanks to private enterprise, backed up somewhat with the city's assistance, from a very small place a few years since, it has grown to its present vast size, and no doubt will keep on growing, its success is mainly due to its unacknowledged distinction of class in society. The rich and the poor, the healthy and invalid are equally well received. All who are bound here for either health or pleasure will find themselves well suited. One of the chief features of Atlantic City is the

BOARD WALK,

which is nearly three miles in length ; it is built on piles on the beach, and affords a splendid promenade and uninterrupted view of the sea.

WOLSIEFFER'S

Circulating Library

Now over **2;700** volumes, and new books added every week. Visitors and guests of Atlantic City, as well as the citizens, will be pleased to know of the opportunity to secure good and cheap reading at this the **Largest Circulating Library in the City**, located in

WOLSIEFFER'S MUSIC AND STATIONERY STORE,

No. 1210 ATLANTIC AVENUE,

Next to Post Office, where also a full line of **Fancy Goods, Novelties, Art Goods**, at Philadelphia prices can be found.

J. HENRY WOLSIEFFER, - ATLANTIC CITY, N. J.

SMITH'S
Atlantic Bakery

ATLANTIC AND OHIO AVENUES,

SOLE AGENT FOR

The Great Food Flour

It is the latest and most important advance in Milling, because it practically recognizes in its manufacturing processes and product, the supreme character and value of Wheat as a human food. Eminent scientists pronounce it

"THE NOBLEST ADDITION TO THE FOODS OF THE WORLD."

BREAD FROM THIS FLOUR BAKED DAILY AND DELIVERED
TO BOARDING HOUSES AND COTTAGES FOR

5 Cents per One lb. Loaf.

OPEN ALL THE YEAR EXCEPT SUNDAY.

The centre mile of the walk, which is opposite the city, well suits the mixed crowd that walks it from morning till night ; such a conglomeration of all classes of society cannot be seen in any other seaside resort in the world. The rich banker does not look down upon the shop boy he meets, and the boy thinks himself equally as good as the banker, for he feels the few dollars in his pocket that he has been so long scraping together to pay the expenses of this visit, and while he smokes his cigar (two for five) he thinks he is indeed doing the grand, and hopes before his week is up to leave, that some millionaire's daughter will take a fancy to him. All along this mile of walk are candy stores, photographers, bath-houses, ice cream saloons, skating rinks, tobacconists, and many other stores and enterprises crowded one on another. The last portion of the walk, that nearest the West Jersey Excursion House, is devoted to things on the cheap. Here you can have your portrait (?) taken eighteen for twenty-five cents ; the genuine Havana cigar, two for five, besides flying horses, combination shows and other amusements too numerous to mention here, and at night all around and overhead glare lights from electric, gas and naphtha lamps, amidst sounds of music from the piers and the beating of the waves on the

I. G. ADAMS.   C. J. ADAMS.

ISRAEL G. ADAMS & CO.

◁REAL ESTATE▷

AND

INSURANCE AGENTS,

2031 ATLANTIC AVENUE, BELOW MICHIGAN,

ATLANTIC CITY, N. J.

Hotels, Cottages, Bath Houses and Lots for sale or rent. Agents for the Chelsea Beach Company, South Atlantic City and Long Port. Farms and Country Residences for sale in Atlantic County, with good ocean view, turnpike, and near West Jersey Railroad station. Any correspondence promptly answered with full particulars.

J. F. HALL.   W. T. CANBY.

HALL & CANBY,

Hotel Advertising Agents

FOR LEADING PAPERS IN

Philadelphia, Baltimore, Washington, Pittsburgh, New York,
Albany, Wilmington, Chester, Williamsport, Harrisburg,
Reading, Chicago and other places.

1630 ATLANTIC AVE., Times Building, ATLANTIC CITY, N. J.

J. V. ALBERTSON,

DEALER IN

Fresh Fish, Oysters and Clams

THE BEST STOCK IN MARKET ALWAYS ON HAND.

TENNESSEE AVENUE, near City Hall, ATLANTIC CITY, N. J.

ELDRIDGE & BURKARD,

DEALERS IN

Meats, Poultry, Eggs, Butter and Game,

CENTRAL MARKET,

COR. MARYLAND AND ATLANTIC AVENUES.

All goods delivered free of charge.   OYSTERS.

PURE MILK   AND CREAM

from the choicest dairies   delivered twice daily to all
of New Jersey,   parts of the City.

DAIRY, 1710 ATLANTIC AVENUE,

Between Illinois and Indiana Avenues, and at

LEEDS' COTTAGE, ARKANSAS AVENUE,

Below Atlantic Avenue.

QUALITY GUARANTEED.   R. H. WILSON.

beach, the crowd tramp on.   No doubt some day someone will say the Board-walk is dreadfully common, and Mrs. Grundy will try to wipe it out, but till that day arrives let those who now visit it enjoy the innocent entertainments provided for them.

HOTEL AND COTTAGE ACCOMMODATIONS

are amply provided to suit the requirements of all that visit Atlantic City.   On pages 4 and 5 will be found a list of hotels, their capacity and rates, and on other pages a full description of leading hotels and cottages that can be recommended.

VISITORS WHO REQUIRE TO DO SHOPPING

will find a complete list of business stores where goods can be purchased equal in quality and at as low a price as in Philadelphia ; these stores we can recommend, see page 7.   For other information respecting Atlantic City, see Contents, page 8.

KIPPLE & McCANN'S HOT SEA-WATER BATHS.
Complete in all their appointments. Robes for Surf Bathing. Open all the year.

SEA-END OF OCEAN AVE.,   ATLANTIC CITY, N. J.

The Most Reasonable Undertaking Establishment in Atlantic City.

JOS. S. CHAMPION,

FUNERAL DIRECTOR

AND

FURNISHING UNDERTAKER,

Office, 1026 Atlantic Avenue, Atlantic City, N. J.

OPEN DAY AND NIGHT.

Velvet Cloth-covered, Rosewood, Oak, Walnut and Metallic Burial Caskets furnished at the shortest notice. Bodies Preserved in Ice. The only one using the Ice Shipping Casket. Ready-made Burial Robes.

The only Funeral Director that makes a specialty of conducting Funerals direct from Atlantic City to any cemetery in Philadelphia or suburbs. Satisfaction guaranteed.

PERSONAL ATTENDANCE AT ALL HOURS.

DUNGAN'S LIVERY STABLE,

OFFICE AND STABLES,

REAR OF TAMMANY AND MANSION HOUSE.

Horses and Carriages of Every Description to Hire at All Hours. Boarding Horses a specialty.

P. O. BOX 493.   **ATLANTIC CITY, N. J.**

The Atlantic Laundry

1505 ATLANTIC AVENUE.

Our work will be done in a first-class manner and at Philadelphia prices. **Collars and Cuffs a specialty.** Goods delivered and collected free of charge. Clothes washed and rinsed in pure spring water. Prompt delivery guaranteed.

P. O. BOX 1127.   CATHRALL BROS.

POST OFFICE DIRECTORY.

MAILS ARRIVE—READY FOR DISTRIBUTION.

From Philadelphia and all points West and South ; New York and all points in Eastern States ; May's Landing and other local mails, 11.30 a. m. From Philadelphia and points West and South, and May's Landing, 6 p. m. From New York and Eastern States ; local mails (New Jersey), 7.00 p. m.

MAILS DEPART—CLOSE AT POST OFFICE.

For Philadelphia and points West and South ; local mails, and New York and Eastern States, 6.40 a. m. For May's Landing 7.15 a. m. For Philadelphia and points East, West and South, May's Landing and local mails, 3.10 p. m.

Post Office open from 6 o'clock a. m. to 8 o'clock p. m.

Sunday Mails.—Arrive at 10.00 a. m. Depart at 3.50 p. m.

Office open on Sunday from 11.00 a. m. to 12 m., and 3.00 to 4.00 p. m. Money Orders issued and paid from 8 a. m. to 5 p. m. Letters and packages registered from 8 a. m. to 5 p. m.

All mails from hotels and boarding houses must be at the Post Office twenty minutes before the time for closing the mails, as above stated. L. C. ALBERTSON, P. M.

Fresh Cut Flowers

Received daily directly from OUR OWN Conservatories. Designs of every description neatly executed at short notice. Flowers of the finest quality constantly kept on hand.

Cor. North Carolina and Pacific Avenues, next to the Colonnade.

DEVOUX EDWARDS, Manager.

We have over one-half acre under glass at our place in Bridgeton, and have every facility for furnishing fancy plants and cut flowers.

S. EDWARDS & SON, Proprietors.

Art Store

C. B. Wilson, 1616 Atlantic Avenue.

Novelties in finely Painted Sea Shells, Plaques, etc.
Rare Shells for Cabinets.
Lessons in Decorated Pottery.
Artists' Materials.

Branch of Wilson's Circulating Library.

APPLEGATE'S

DOUBLE-DECKED PIER

AND

Branch Galleries

——————ARE NOW OPEN——————

The Pier is nicely enclosed with a tight roof, sash and glass,—perfectly safe from both wind and rain,—affording a walk over the waves of almost 1,200 feet on one of the most substantial structures on the coast, and will stand the weight of 20,000 people.

Admission, Day or Night, to all Decks, 5 cts.
Baby Carriages Free.

The Fishing Deck can accommodate 500 persons, and is the coolest and most extensive concern on the coast.

OUR GALLERIES in connection with the *Double-Deck Pier* (and a Branch of our immense Galleries in Philadelphia), is the *most extensive Likeness concern* at any seaside resort in the world.

> Atlantic City by the Sea,
> Where thousands go to rusticate,
> And wishing first-class pictures made,
> In Crowds drop in to APPLEGATE.

Patrons of the Galleries admitted to the Pier
FREE OF CHARGE.

RELIGIOUS NOTICES.

CHURCH OF THE ASCENSION, Atlantic City, N. J. Order of services from Easter, 1885, to Ash Wednesday, 1886: Sundays—celebration of Holy Communion, 7.30 a. m.; Morning Prayer, Litany and Sermon, 11.00 a. m.; Sunday School, 3.30 p. m.; Choral Service and Catechising, 4.00 p. m.; Evening Prayer, &c., 8 p. m. First Sunday of the month—Morning Prayer, 10.30 a. m.; Litany, Sermon and Second Celebration, 11 a. m. Saints Days—Celebration of Holy Communion, 7.30 a. m. Wednesdays—Litany and Bible Study, 8 p. m. Fridays—Litany and Meditation or Instruction, 10 a. m. Special notice given of Lenten and other extra services. The church is on Pacific ave., west of Michigan. Open all the year. All seats free at every service.

FIRST PRESBYTERIAN CHURCH, Pacific avenue, corner of Pennsylvania avenue, Rev. William Aikman, D. D., pastor. Preaching services on Sunday at 10.30 a. m. and 8 p. m. Sabbath School and Bible Classes, 3 p. m. Regular church prayer meeting and lecture Wednesday evening at 8 p. m.

GERMAN PRESBYTERIAN CHURCH, corner of Pacific and Ocean avenues. Services every Sunday at 10.30 a. m. and 7.30 p. m. Sunday School at 2.30 p. m. Prayer meeting Wednesday evening at 7.30 o'clock. Catechetical instruction Tuesday at 4.15. Rev. A. W. Fismer, pastor; residence, 26 West Maryland avenue.

ST. PAUL'S METHODIST EPISCOPAL CHURCH, Arctic avenue, corner of Ohio. Rev. G. S. Meseroll, pastor. Preaching services Sunday at 10.30 a. m. and 7.30 p. m. Sabbath School 2.30 p. m. Prayer meeting on Thursday evening at 7.30.

SEASIDE HOUSE,

Sea-End of Pennsylvania Avenue, Atlantic City, N. J.

Situated on the highest point of ground in Atlantic City. Facing and in full view of the ocean. Thoroughly heated in Winter. Lighted with gas. Electric Bells, Billiard and Reading Rooms, etc. OPEN PERMANENTLY. **CHARLES EVANS.**

ATLANTIC CITY, N. J.

OPEN ALL THE YEAR.

This house has been furnished with all modern improvements to insure comfort to those visiting the Seashore. Steam, Gas, Electric Bells, Spring and Hair Mattresses in every room, large and attractive Parlors, Billiard, Smoking and Sitting Rooms on First Floor. Hot and Cold Sea-water Baths in the House, Perfect Sewerage. Delightful location, convenient to all places of interest on the Seashore, and nearest first-class House to Depots, only one block distant. The present proprietor having large experience in First-Class Hotel catering feels that he cannot be surpassed as a Caterer and the excellence of Cuisine. Those desiring to make special arrangements for Board or information concerning the advantages of Atlantic City over other Seaside Resorts as a Winter Sanitarium, will please apply at the Hotel, or by letter to

NO BAR.   **C. C. LEFLER & CO.**

RELIGIOUS NOTICES—*Continued.*

FIRST M. E. CHURCH, Atlantic avenue above Connecticut. Rev. John H. Boswell, pastor. Preaching every Sunday at 10.30 a. m. and 7.30 p. m. Sunday school at 2 p. m. Prayer meeting Wednesday evening at 7.30. Teachers' Bible Study, Saturday evening at 8 o'clock.

METHODIST PROTESTANT CHURCH, corner of Baltic and Michigan aves. Rev. R. G. Patterson, pastor. Preaching Sundays at 10.30 a. m. and 8 p.m. Prayer meeting, Tuesday evening, at 7.30.

FIRST BAPTIST CHURCH, Pacific avenue, near North Carolina. Rev. Wm. E. Boyle, D. D., pastor. Services: preaching on Sunday morning at 10.30, evening at 7.30. Sabbath School at 2.30 p. m. Prayer meeting Friday evening at 7.45.

ST. NICHOLAS' CHURCH, Atlantic below Tennessee. Rev. J. J. Fedigan, O. S. A., pastor. Order of divine services: Every Sunday and Holy Day, Mass (Sundays) June, 6.30 and 9.30; July and August, 5.30, 6.30, 8.30, 9.30; rest of the year, 7.30 and 9.30; on every Holy Day, 8. Vespers Sunday evenings at 7.30. Sunday School always at 2 p. m. All other services in the chapel, cor. Tennessee and Pacific Avenues, every morning during the season, 7 a. m. Confessions Saturday from 3 to 9 p. m., or whenever requested.

FRIENDS' MEETING HOUSE, corner of Pacific and South Carolina avenues. Services at 10.30 every First-day, under the direction of the Haddonfield Monthly Meeting.

BETHEL A. M. E. CHURCH, Baltic, above Maryland avenue. Rev. J. T. Rex, pastor. Services every Sunday at 10.30 a. m. and 8 p.m. Sunday School at 2.30 p.m. Prayer meeting, Tuesday at 8 p.m.

THE "MARGATE,"
(FIRST SEASON)
COR. PACIFIC AND SURF AVES.

Open all the Year.   Large Rooms.   Ocean View.   Newly Furnished.

SAM'L. KIRBY, Proprietor, (late of the Seaside House.)

Atlantic City.

UNDER NEW MANAGEMENT.

Kelsey & Lefler, Proprietors.

See Advertisement of Stockton Cafe.

Stockton Cafe,

ADJOINING AND CONNECTED WITH

The Stockton Hotel,

FOR LADIES AND GENTLEMEN,

Atlantic Avenue, Corner of Maryland Avenue,

Atlantic City, N. J.

This is the finest and best-appointed Restaurant in Atlantic City; re-furnished and re-fitted throughout; where meals or dishes to order can be obtained at all hours, including eatables of every variety in season, served in a strictly first-class manner at short notice, and at moderate prices, either in the Restaurant, Dining Rooms, or in Private Rooms, connected with the Cafe, handsomely furnished for the purpose. Parties so desiring can have Private Dining Rooms. Attached to the Cafe is a first-class Sample Room.   **KELSEY & LEFLER.**

TIDE TABLE.

HIGH WATER AT ATLANTIC CITY.

	JUNE			JULY			AUGUST	
	A.M.	P.M.		A.M.	P.M.		A.M.	P.M.
Mon. 1.	9.47	10.00	Wed. 1.	10.00	10.13	Sat. 1.	10.46	11.07
Tue. 2.	10.21	10.43	Thu. 2.	10.33	11.00	Sun. 2.	11.28	11.51
Wed. 3.	11.04	11.24	Fri. 3.	11.15	11.35	Mon. 3.	12.14	12.38
Thu. 4.	11.44	12.06	Sat. 4.	12.00	12.18	Tue. 4.	1.06	1.37
Fri. 5.	12.28	1.01	Sun. 5.	12.43	1.06	Wed. 5.	2.12	2.49
Sat. 6.	1.15	1.42	Mon. 6.	1.34	2.04	Thu. 6.	3.24	4.00
Sun. 7.	2.12	2.41	Tue. 7.	2.37	3.11	Fri. 7.	4.35	5.09
Mon. 8.	3.11	3.42	Wed. 8.	3.45	4.19	Sat. 8.	5.42	5.51
Tue. 9.	4.12	4.43	Thu. 9.	5.00	5.26	Sun. 9.	6.12	6.41
Wed. 10.	5.15	5.45	Fri. 10.	5.47	6.00	Mon. 10.	7.06	7.30
Thu. 11.	6.00	6.14	Sat. 11.	6.27	7.00	Tue. 11.	7.45	8.20
Fri. 12.	64.1	7.08	Sun. 12.	7.22	8.00	Wed. 12.	8.44	9.08
Sat. 13.	7.35	8.02	Mon. 13.	8.15	8.41	Thu. 13.	9.31	9.43
Sun. 14.	8.30	9.00	Tue. 14.	9.06	9.31	Fri. 14.	10.16	10.38
Mon. 15.	9.24	10.00	Wed. 15.	10.00	10.20	Sat. 15.	11.00	11.22
Tue. 16.	10.16	10.42	Thu. 16.	10.43	11.06	Sun. 16.	11.44	12.07
Wed. 17.	11.07	11.31	Fri. 17.	11.28	11.51	Mon. 17.	12.30	12.55
Thu. 18.	12.00	12.18	Sat. 18.	12.14	12.37	Tue. 18.	1.23	1.58
Fri. 19.	12.42	1.08	Sun. 19.	1.02	1.28	Wed. 19.	2.19	2.58
Sat. 20.	1.36	2.04	Mon. 20.	2.00	2.16	Thu. 20.	3.18	3.47
Sun. 21.	2.33	3.02	Tue. 21.	3.00	3.24	Fri. 21.	4.15	4.43
Mon. 22.	3.31	4.00	Wed. 22.	4.00	4.26	Sat. 22.	5.09	5.33
Tue. 23.	4.27	5.00	Thu. 23.	4.51	5.15	Sun. 23.	5.47	5.56
Wed. 24.	5.18	5.33	Fri. 24.	5.40	5.48	Mon. 24.	6.19	6.40
Thu. 25.	5.48	6.07	Sat. 25.	6.04	6.37	Tue. 25.	6.53	7.18
Fri. 26.	6.30	7.00	Sun. 26.	6.47	7.06	Wed. 26.	7.37	8.00
Sat. 27.	7.20	7.30	Mon. 27.	7.25	7.45	Thu. 27.	8.17	8.37
Sun. 28.	8.00	8.13	Tue. 28.	8.06	8.26	Fri. 28.	9.00	9.17
Mon. 29.	8.33	9.00	Wed. 29.	8.45	9.05	Sat. 29.	9.38	10.00
Tue. 30.	9.14	9.34	Thu. 30.	9.25	9.44	Sun. 30.	10.20	10.33
			Fri. 31.	10.04	10.25	Mon. 31.	11.07	11.31

THE "EDGEWATER,"

South Carolina Avenue, below Pacific,

ATLANTIC CITY, N. J.

OPEN ALL THE YEAR. FINE OCEAN VIEW. CONVENIENT TO THE
BOARD WALK, RAILWAY DEPOTS AND HOT BATHS.

P. O. Box 930.   E. D. PARKINSON.

UNITED STATES HOTEL

ATLANTIC CITY, N. J.

Opens
June 27th.
—
Leading
Hotel.
—
Superb
Appointments.

Excellent
Cuisine.
—
Electric
Bells.
—
Fire Escape,
etc., etc.

LAWN VIEW.

BENJ. H. BROWN, Proprietor.   W. WHITNEY, Manager.

CARRIAGES AND HORSES FOR HIRE.

Carriage with 2 horses, with driver,	-	-	-	$1 50 per hour.
" " 2 " without driver,	-	-	-	2 00 " "
" " 1 horse, " "	-	-	-	1 00 " "
Cart " 1 " " "	-	-	-	1 50 " "
Saddle horses,	-	-	-	-	-	-	-	1 00 " "
Carriages to and from R. R. Depot,	-	-	-	50 " "

Street cars from Inlet to Excursion House, (West Jersey), along Atlantic Avenue, fare 6 cents.

BATHING RATES, ETC.

Hot Sea Water Baths, 50 cents.   Three tickets for $1.00.
Surf Baths, with bathing suit, 25 cents.
Surf Baths, with your own bathing suit, 50 cents per week.

BOATS FOR HIRE,

According to size of boat and number of persons, from 25 cents to $1.00 per hour.

HADDON HOUSE,

WINTER AND SUMMER,

Sea-End of North Carolina Avenue, Atlantic City, N. J.

EDWIN LIPPINCOTT.

OCEAN HOUSE,
COR. PACIFIC AND CONNECTICUT AVES.

Open Summer and Winter.   Fine Ocean View.   Heated by Steam and Open Grate Fire.
Gas and Electric Bells   Hot and Cold Sea Water Baths in the house.

J. A. REID, Proprietor.

THE CLARENDON,
Ocean End of Virginia Avenue, Atlantic City, N. J.

Fine location, on high ground, commanding an extended view of the ocean   Board
walk to the beach. Open all the year.

Col. JOHN M. CLARK, Proprietor.

THE THEATRES.

THE VIRGINIA OPERA COMIQUE, has just been built on the site of the Virginia Gardens in Virginia avenue, and seats nearly 2000 people, it has a fine stage and roomy dressing rooms for the performers, while the comfort of its visitors has been thoroughly looked after. Messrs. Morton & Southwell, of Haverly's Theatre, Philadelphia, are the proprietors and managers. McCaull's Opera Company has been engaged. With such managers and opera company, the Virginia Opera Comique cannot fail to be a great success.

THE IDEAL OPERA HOUSE, situated at corner of Kentucky and Atlantic avenues, should the weather be fine, no doubt will be well patronized, for its roof and sides are of canvas. It seats nearly 2000 persons. It is devoted to opera.

THE THEATRE in Pavilion attached to the Mansion House, has been fitted up for the production of light drama during the months of July and August. The Pavilion has been entirely roofed in and the stage enlarged. Messrs. C. McGlade and William Davidge, Jr., the actor, are the proprietors and managers.

THE LIGHT HOUSE.

THE ABSECON LIGHT HOUSE is at Ocean end of Vermont avenue. It is 167 feet high to centre of lantern. Its fixed white light can been seen 20 miles at sea. The light house is built of brick and hydraulic cement. Admission, free of charge. Open between the hours of 9 a. m. and 12 m.

HOTEL ROYAL,

KENTUCKY AND PACIFIC AVENUES,

ATLANTIC CITY, N. J.

THIS new and elegantly-appointed hotel, under the management of J. F. CAKE, of Old Congress Hall, Cape May, and Willard's Hotel, Washington. Will be open all the year. All modern improvements, electric bells, steam heating, etc.

THE CHALFONTE

Ocean End of North Carolina Avenue.

THOROUGHLY RENOVATED GAS NEW FURNITURE, WARDROBES,
ETC., ETC.

NOW OPEN.   **ELISHA ROBERTS & SON.**

ATLANTIC CITY.

THE CHESTER COUNTY HOUSE

IS NOW OPEN.

This well-known house, in the twenty fifth season of successful management by its
present owners, again invites Summer visitors. Within a few hundred feet of
the sea, it is one of the coolest and most comfortable seashore homes.

J. KEIM & SONS.

EMERSON HOUSE,

South Carolina Avenue, near the Ocean,

ATLANTIC CITY, N. J.

This house has been enlarged, newly papered and is furnished with gas, electric bells,
and thoroughly heated for a Winter house. The rooms are large and well
ventilated. It is within one half square of the Hot Baths and Ocean

Telephone 93.   **DuBOIS & YOUNG, Proprietors.**

THE ELBERON,

Cor. Pacific and Tennessee Aves.

COMPLETE IN ALL ITS APPOINTMENTS. UNDER NEW MANAGEMENT.

Open all the year.   **L. A. ROWAN.**

THE RAILWAYS.

TO OR FROM PHILADELPHIA.

To **Atlantic City.**—Fares, single or excursion ticket, (10 days return) $1.50.

By Pennsylvania and West Jersey R. R., Market Street Ferry.

By Camden and Atlantic R. R., Vine Street Ferry.

Or by Philadelphia and Atlantic City R. W., single or excursion ticket, (ten days return) $1.00, from Pier 8, below Walnut street.

To **Philadelphia.**—Single or excursion ticket (10 days return) $1.00, per Camden and Atlantic R. R.; returning by either Camden and Atlantic or Pennsylvania and West Jersey R. R. ¶

LIFE SAVING STATION.

THE U. S. LIFE SAVING STATION situated close to light house. It has large, swift surf boat and all the modern appliances to save life at sea. There are eight men and the keeper connected with the station. Admission, free to visitors.

ASHLAND HOUSE,

COR. PENNSYLVANIA AND ATLANTIC AVENUES,

IS NOW OPEN.

First-class Appointments, Location and Cuisine with moderate charges.

Mrs. M. S. LOCKWOOD.

ASHLAND HOUSE RESTAURANT

AND

ICE CREAM SALOON AND PARLORS,

djoining the Ashland House Hotel. Here visitors will find their comforts strictly attended to.

THE WETHERILL,

Ocean End of Kentucky Avenue, 100 yards from the beach, Atlantic City, N. J.

P. O. Box No. 7. **Mrs. CAROLINE F. WILSON,**

OPEN ALL THE YEAR. Owner and Proprietress.

Mrs Wilson's former success in this line is a guarantee as to the standing of the house.

THE HYGEIA,
COR. NEW YORK and PACIFIC AVENUES.

Fronting and near the Ocean. Fine Location. House new and nicely furnished.
Superior accommodations. Terms moderate.

OPEN ALL THE YEAR.   **Mrs. E. A. STAVRO.**

THE ALDINE,
Pacific below Ohio Avenue, Atlantic City, N. J.

The Aldine is pleasantly situated near the Beach, with full Ocean view. Terms
moderate and home comforts.

Lock Box 19.   **JAMES HOOD.**

THE DUDLEY ARMS,
PENNSYLVANIA AVENUE,

Is now open under new management. Fine Location. Complete Appointments.
Faultless Cuisine. Good attendance.

City Address, 359 N. 15th St.   **M. P. KIRK.**

LANSDALE HOUSE,
39 North Carolina Ave., Atlantic City, N. J.

Open all the year. One square between the Ocean and the Railroad Depot.

Mrs. I. JOHNSTON, Proprietress.

THE LANCASTER,
SOUTH CAROLINA AVENUE.

Open all the Year. Full Ocean View. Handsomely Furnished. Homelike Comforts.
Within Fifty yards of the Beach, Piers, and Hot Baths.

Address, P. O. Box 873.   **Mrs. M. J. KUNKLE, Proprietress.**

THE WESTMINSTER,
Cor. Pacific and Kentucky Avenues.

Full ocean view. Close to beach, piers, stores, etc. Under new management.
Terms moderate.

Mrs. MARY ROCHE, (Late of Linwood Cottage.)

THE CONTINENTAL,
Atlantic above Rhode Island Avenue, Atlantic City, N. J

This favorite house is nicely furnished, with thoroughly heated rooms, and broad piazzas
overlooking the ocean. It is situated in one of the most delightful locations on the island,
being in close proximity to the beach, lighthouse and hot and cold sea water baths, and
is now open for the reception of permanent and transient guests at reduced prices.

P. O. Box 271.   **Mrs. S. HITCHENS**

LEED'S COTTAGE,
Arkansas Avenue, below Atlantic, Atlantic City, N. J.

Opposite Narrow Gauge Depot.

TERMS MODERATE.   **Mrs. R. H. WILSON**

THE PIERS.

APPLEGATE'S DOUBLE-DECK PIER is situated at end of Tennessee avenue. It is 625 feet in length. In the Pavilion at the end of pier a series of concerts, minstrel performances, etc., are given. Excellent fishing can be had from off the head of the pier. Admission, 5 cents. See page 24.

HOWARD'S PIER, end of Kentucky avenue, is said to be 600 feet in length. Its chief attractions are a skating rink and concerts. Admission, 10 cents.

A NEW IRON PIER at the Inlet end of Atlantic City will shortly be commenced. It will be 1000 feet in length, from which steamers can land their passengers. The Phœnix Iron Co. are the contractors, which will be a guarantee as to the fine material used and workmanship.

SKATING RINKS.

THE VICTORIA, Sea end of South Carolina avenue. This skating rink is 150 ft. in length by 60 ft. broad, and by its good management, its series of first-class professional contests and performances, by its fine band of music, and courtesy shown all who visit it by its officials, has gained well deserved patronage. Miss Williams, of the Victoria Hotel, is the proprietress. Admission, 10 cents in the day ; 20 cents at night. Saturday, 20 cents.

SKATING RINK on Howard's Pier. This rink has been recently built by the proprietors, Messrs. Clark & Ryan, the well-known sporting caterers of amusements in Philadelphia. Admission, 10 cts.

ALBRECHT'S SKATING RINK and Summer Garden, 1716 Atlantic avenue.

OCEAN VILLA,

Cor. South Carolina and Pacific Aves., Atlantic City, N. J.

Heated thoroughly. Open permanently. Terms moderate, with home comforts. Convenient to depots and beach.

P. O. Box 790. **Mrs. S. M. PRICE, Proprietress.**

REVERE HOUSE,

(Opposite The Brighton,)

ATLANTIC CITY, N. J.

Park Place, below Pacific, and between Indiana and Ohio Avenues, half square from the Ocean.

OPEN ALL THE YEAR. **M. DAY.**

THE RENOVO,

OPEN ALL THE YEAR,

Tennessee Avenue, Second House from the Beach, Atlantic City, N. J.

One square from Applegate's Pier and W. J. R. R. Depot.

P. O. Box 266. **R. W. CLEAVER.**

THE RADNOR,

South Carolina Avenue, near Ocean, Atlantic City, N. J.

P. O. Box 1030. **Mrs. M. J. ECKERT.**

Why not Get the Best?

JAS. SMITH & SON'S

TRADE   MARK

NEEDLES

JAMES SMITH & SON have the honor to inform ladies and the public generally, that they were the only British firm of Needle Manufacturers which received from the Commission of the Centennial Exhibition, Philadelphia, 1876, the distinction of TWO awards.

SEE JUDGES' REPORT.

THINGS YOU OUGHT TO KNOW

Valuable and Useful Information,

AND A

RELIABLE SHOPPING GUIDE.

ONE of the most important things for all house-keepers to know is where to buy the BEST BEEF for the LEAST MONEY.

CALL AT

THOMAS BRADLEY'S

GREAT WESTERN

Meat Market

N. W. CORNER

TWENTY-FIRST AND MARKET STREETS,

AND YOU WILL BE CONVINCED THAT THIS IS THE PLACE.

We handle everything in the Meat line, including Spring Lamb, Southdown Mutton, Hams, Lard, Dried Beef, Tongues, etc.; have our cattle killed in Chicago and shipped direct to us in refrigerator cars, consequently it eats much better than when killed here. We have the very best facilities for handling the beef in a proper manner (as a visit will convince you). We do our utmost to give satisfaction and will be pleased to have you call.

OPEN SATURDAY NIGHTS UNTIL TEN O'CLOCK.

CONTENTS.

SHOPPING GUIDE.

Good Old-Fashioned Soap.

WE are now and have been making for many years two OLD-FASHIONED SOAPS, made, as we believe, proper and perfect for the purpose that Soap is intended for—to cleanse and purify, without injury to the skin or clothing.

Family Soap, for Washing Clothes,

Price, 8 cents per pound,   **Boxes of fifty pounds.**

Palm Soap, for Bath and Toilet,

Price, $1.25 per dozen.   **and 30 cts. per pound.**

⇒FOR THE BATH AND TOILET⇐
USE
OUR PURE PALM OIL SOAP.

This Soap is made of Pure Fresh Palm Oil, and is entirely a vegetable Soap, more suitable for Toilet use than Soap made from animal fats.

LINDLEY M. ELKINTON,

532 St. John Street,   *PHILADELPHIA, PA.*

ANNUAL SALARIES OF THE PRINCIPAL MILITARY AND CIVIL OFFICERS OF THE U. S.

President	$50,000	Brigadier General	$5,500
Vice-President	10,000	Colonels	5,300
Secretary of State	8,000	Lieutenant Colonels	3,000
" " Treasury	8,000	Majors	2,500
" " Interior	8,000	Captains	1,800 to 2,000
" " War	8,000	1st Lieutenants	1,500 to 1,600
" " Navy	8,000	2d Lieutenants	1,400 to 1,500
Postmaster General	8,000	Admirals of Navy	13,000
Attorney General	8,000	Vice Admirals	9,000
Speaker of the House of Representatives	8,000	Rear Admirals	6,000
U. S. Senators	5,000	Commodore	5,000
Represent's in Congress	5,000	Captains of Navy	4,500
Judges Supreme Court	10,000	Commanders	3,500
Associate Judges	10,000	1st Lieutenants	2,800
General of the Army	13,000	2d Lieutenants	2,500
Lieutenant General	11,000	Masters	1,800
Major General	7,500	Engineers	1,200
		Midshipmen	1,000

President...............GROVER CLEVELAND...........of New Jersey
Salary, $50,000.

Vice-President..........THOS. A. HENDRICKS................of Indiana
Salary, $10,000.

Secretary of State.........THOMAS F. BAYARD....................of Delaware
Secretary of Treasury....DANIEL MANNING....................of New York
Secretary of War..........WILLIAM C. ENDICOTT.........of Massachusetts
Secretary of Navy........WILLIAM C. WHITNEY..............of New York
Secretary of Interior.....L. Q. C. LAMAR....................of Mississippi
Postmaster General......WILLIAM F. VILAS...................of Wisconsin
Attorney General........AUGUSTUS H. GARLAND..............of Arkansas
Salary, $8,000 each.

AVERAGE VELOCITY OF ELEMENTS AND OBJECTS.

Electricity	288,000	miles	a second.
Sight	12,200	"	"
Rifle Ball	1,000	"	an hour.
Sound	743	"	"
Hurricane moves	80	"	"
Storm moves	36	"	"
Horse runs	20	"	"
Steamboat	18	"	"
Sailing vessel	10	"	"
Rapid river flows	7	"	"
Moderate wind blows	7	"	"

Richard S. Groves.   Henry Steil.

R. S. Groves & Steil,

Manufacturers of

Stained, Embossed, Enameled

and

Cut Glass,

Modern and Antique Glass for Churches. Imperishable Ornamented Glass Tiles for Flooring, Fire Places, and Mantels, Vestibules, Outside and Inside Decorations. Portraits to Order. Housework a Specialty. Designs and Estimates Furnished on Application. Opalescent Glass and Jewels.

Philadelphia

Stained Glass Works,

Nos. 617 South Broad St., and 1348 Kater St.,

Philadelphia.

PHILADELPHIA CITY OFFICERS.

Mayor,
WILLIAM B. SMITH, *R.*

Salary, $5,000.   Term Expires, April, 1887.

City Solicitor,
CHARLES F. WARWICK, *R.*

Salary, $10,000.   Term Expires, April, 1887.

Receiver of Taxes,
JOHN HUNTER, *I. R.*

Salary, $2,500 and commissions.   Term Expires, April, 1887.

PHILADELPHIA COUNTY OFFICERS.

Controller.
COL. ROBERT P. DECHERT, *D.*

Salary, $8,000.   Term Expires, Jan., 1888.

Treasurer,
WILLIAM B. IRVINE, *R.*

Salary, $10,000.   Term Expires, Jan., 1886.

Commissioners,
WM. LAWSON, *R.*
WM. S. DOUGLASS, *R.*
CHAS. H. KRUMBHAAR, *D.*

Salary, $5,000 each.   Term Expires, Jan., 1888.

Sheriff,
GEO. DEB. KEIM, *R.*

Salary, $15,000.   Term Expires, Jan., 1886.

Recorder of Deeds,
GEORGE G. PIERIE, *R.*

Salary, $10,000.   Term Expires, Jan., 1888.

District Attorney,
GEO. S. GRAHAM, *R.*

Salary, $10,000.   Term Expires, Jan., 1887.

Register of Wills,
WALTER E. REX, *I. R.*

Salary, $10,000.   Term Expires, Jan., 1886.

Clerk of Quarter Sessions,
WILLIAM E. LITTLETON, *R.*

Salary, $5,000.   Term Expires, Jan., 1887.

Coroner,
THOS. J. POWERS, *R.*

Salary, $5,000.   Term Expires, Jan., 1887.

Distance around the world, including the principal stopping places, in a direct line, starting from New York:

New York to San Francisco	3,450	miles
San Francisco to Yokohama	4,764	"
Yokohama to Hong Kong	1,630	"
Hong Kong to Singapore	1,150	"
Singapore to Calcutta	1,200	"
Calcutta to Bombay	1,409	"
Bombay to Aden	1,664	"
Aden to Suez	1,208	"
Suez to Alexandria	250	"
Alexandria to Marseilles	1,300	"
Marseilles to Paris	536	"
Paris to London	316	"
London to Liverpool	205	"
Liverpool to New York	3,000	"
New York to Philadelphia	98	"

⇢American Spool Cotton.⇠

AMERICAN MACHINES.

All the Honors.

America Ahead!

SIX CORD
THE BEST THREAD for SEWING MACHINES.
SPOOL COTTON

Atlanta, 1881.

AMERICAN CAPITAL.

ASK FOR IT! BUY IT!! TRY IT!!!
DO NOT FORGET IT!

⇢See Exhibit at New Orleans.⇠

RATES OF POSTAGE.

LETTERS, ETC.   *Each ½ ounce.*

Mail letters..2 cents.
Drop letters at letter carrier offices.........................2 "
Drop letters at non-letter carrier offices....................1 "
   Drawings, plans, designs and all matter sealed against inspection, 2 cents each ½ oz. or fraction oz.
   Registered letters, 10 cents in addition to the proper postage.
   Second-Class Matter.—Newspapers and periodicals to regular subscribers, quarterly or oftener, 2 cents a lb.
   Transient newspapers, 1 cent each 4 oz.
   Third-Class Matter.—Books (printed and blank), circulars, other printed matter, proof sheets, corrected proof sheets and manuscript, copy accompanying same, valentines, heliotypes, chromos, posters, lithographs, 1 cent each 2 oz.
   Newspapers (except weeklies to subscribers), circulars and periodicals, not 2 oz. in weight, deposited in letter carrier offices for local delivery, 1 cent each.
   Fourth-Class Matter.—Printed envelopes in quantity, blank bills, letter heads, blank cards, flexible patterns, plain envelopes and letter paper, sample cards, merchandise, models, sample ores, metals, minerals, seeds, cuttings, bulbs, roots, not exceeding 4 lbs. in weight, 1 cent each oz. or fraction of oz.
   Patterns and samples to Canada 10 cents prepaid for each 8 oz. or fraction.
   First, third and fourth-class matter may be **registered** at 10 cents each package in addition to regular postage.
   All matter not prepaid at letter rates must be so wrapped that it can be examined without destroying the wrapper, and can name contents, from whom, and address, and nothing more. A business card may be printed, impressed, or pasted on the wrappers. Liquids, poisons, explosives, and other dangerous matters are excluded.

MONEY ORDERS.

   No fractions of cents allowed in any money order.
   Rates on money orders in United States :

On orders not exceeding $10, 8 cts.		Over $50 to $60.................30 cts.
Over $10 to $15.................10 "		" 60 " 70.................35 "
" 15 " 30.................15 "		" 70 " 80.................40 "
" 30 " 40.................20 "		" 80 " 100.................45 "
" 40 " 50.................25 "		

   Money orders to Great Britain or Ireland. Not exceeding $10, twenty-five cents; over $10 to $20, fifty cents; over $20 to $30, seventy cents; over $30 to $40, eighty-five cents; over $40 to $50, one dollar.
   Money orders to German Empire, France, Italy, Canada, Algeria, Switzerland, Jamaica, New Zealand, New South Wales, Victoria, Belgium, Portugal, Hawaii, Queenland, Cape Colony, Windward Islands, and Tasmania : Not exceeding $10, fifteen cents; over $10 to $20, thirty cents; over $20 to $30, forty-five cents; over $30 to $40, sixty cents; over $40 to $50, seventy-five cents
   Money orders can be made payable in Denmark, Sweden and Norway, Netherlands and Luxemburg, through Germany, at German rates. In Austria and Hungary, through Switzerland, at Swiss rates. To India, not exceeding $10, thirty-five cents; over $10 to $20, seventy cents; over $20 to $30, $1; over $30 to $40, $1.25; over $40 to $50, $1.50.
   Postal notes are furnished by any postmaster for any amount under $5, at a cost of three cents each.

POPULATION OF CITIES OF THE UNITED STATES
OVER 100,000.

	Inhabitants.
New York, N. Y	1,206,299
Philadelphia, Pa.	847,170
Brooklyn, N. Y	566,663
Chicago, Ill.	503,185
Boston, Mass.	362,839
St. Louis, Mo.	350,518
Baltimore, Md.	332,313
Cincinnati, O.	255,139
San Francisco, Cal.	233,959
New Orleans, La.	216,090
Cleveland, O.	160,146
Pittsburgh, Pa.	156,389
Buffalo, N. Y.	155,134
Washington, D. C.	147,293
Newark, N. J.	136,508
Louisville, Ky.	123,758
Jersey City, N. J.	120,722
Detroit, Mich.	116,340
Milwaukee, Wis.	115,587
Providence, R. I.	104,857

STEAM HEATING

IN ALL ITS BRANCHES, FOR

Public or Private Buildings.

WOOD'S

American Kitchener

→RANGE←

Particular attention paid to Ventilating by most approved methods.

JAMES P. WOOD & CO.

No. 39 South Fourth Street, Philadelphia, Pa.

AREA AND POPULATION OF THE UNITED STATES.

State.	Square Miles.	Population.
Alabama	50,722	1,262,505
Arkansas	52,198	802,525
California	188,981	864,694
Colorado	104,500	194,327
Connecticut	4,750	622,700
Delaware	2,120	146,608
Florida	59,268	268,493
Georgia	58,000	1,542,180
Illinois	55,410	3,077,871
Indiana	33,809	1,978,301
Iowa	55,045	1,624,615
Kansas	81,318	996,096
Kentucky	37,680	1,648,690
Louisiana	41,346	939,946
Maine	35,000	648,936
Maryland	11,124	934,943
Massachusetts	7,800	1,783,085
Michigan	56,451	1,636,937
Minnesota	83,531	780,773
Mississippi	47,156	1,131,597
Missouri	65,350	2,168,380
Nebraska	75,995	452,402
Nevada	104,125	62,266
New Hampshire	9,280	346,991
New Jersey	8,320	1,131,116
New York	47,000	5,082,871
North Carolina	50,704	1,399,750
Ohio	39,964	3,198,062
Oregon	95,274	174,768
Pennsylvania	46,000	4,282,891
Rhode Island	1,306	276,531
South Carolina	34,000	995,577
Tennessee	45,600	1,542,359
Texas	274,356	1,591,749
Vermont	10,212	332,286
Virginia	38,348	1,512,565
West Virginia	23,000	618,457
Wisconsin	53,924	1,315,497
	2,088,967	49,371,430

AREA AND POPULATION OF THE UNITED STATES TERRITORIES.

Territories.	Square Miles.	Population.
Arizona	113,916	40,440
Dakota	150,932	135,177
District of Columbia	64	177,624
Idaho	86,294	32,610
Montana	143,776	39,159
New Mexico	121,201	119,565
Utah	84,476	143,963
Washington	69,994	75,116
Wyoming	97,883	20,789
Indian	68,991	
Alaska	577,390	30,146
Territories	1,514,917	814,589
States	2,088,967	49,371,430
Total	3,603,884	50,186,019

LANGUAGES SPOKEN.

English language is spoken by	97,000,000
Spanish " " "	72,000,000
German " " "	53,000,000
French " " "	48,000,000

R. G. DeGINTHER,

Flour,

No. 909 North Broad Street,

PHILADELPHIA.

THE LARGEST CITIES IN THE WORLD.

	Census.	Population.
London, England		4,764,000
Paris, France		2,260,000
Pekin, China	Estimated	1,650,000
Canton, China	Estimated	1,500,000
Constantinople, Turkey	1870	1,500,000
New York, U. S. N. A.	1880	1,206,299
Berlin, Germany	1880	1,122,385
Singan fu, China	1875 estimated	1,000,000
Tschantschan fu, China	1875 estimated	1,000,000
Philadelphia, U. S. N. A.	1880	847,170
Vienna, Austria	1880	726,105
Calcutta, India	1881	683,329
St. Petersburg, Russia	1880	667,963
Bombay, India	1872	644,405
Moscow, Russia	1871	601,959
Bangkok, India	Estimated	600,000
Too Chow, China	Estimated	600,000
Hunkow, China	Estimated	600,000
Tokio, Japan	1877	594,284
Brooklyn, U. S. N. A.	1880	566,663
Glasgow, Scotland	1881	555,289
Liverpool, England	1881	522,425
Chicago, U. S. N. A.	1880	503,985
Naples, Italy	1878	450,804
Birmingham, England	1881	400,759

The longest Rivers **are**: Amazon, 3,944 miles, South America ; Hoang Ho, 2,500 miles, China ; Mirry, 3,000 miles, Australia ; Obi, 2,800 miles, Siberia ; Nile, 2,750 miles, Egypt ; Missouri, 4,194 miles, United States. Volga, 2,000 miles ; Yang-tse-Kiang, 3,000 miles ; Amoor, 2,000 miles ; St. Lawrence, 2,200 miles.

There are 2,950 miles of canals **in the** United States, **the longest being** the Wabash and Erie, 496 miles.

INLAND SEAS OF THE WORLD.

Name.	Size
Caspian Sea	176,000 square miles.
Sea of Aral	30,000 "
Dead Sea	303 "
Lake Baikal	12,000 "
Lake Superior	32,000 "
Lake Michigan	22,400 "
Lake Huron	21,000 "
Lake Erie	10,815 "
Lake Ontario	6,300 "
Lake Nicaragua	6,000 "
Lake Titacaca	3,012 "
Salt Lake	1,875 "
Lake Tchad	14,900 "
Lake Ladoga	12,000 "

POPULATION OF THE EARTH, &c.

	Square Miles.	Population	To Square Miles.
America	14,700,000	95,495,500	6½
Europe	3,800,000	315,929,000	83
Asia	15,000,000	834,707,000	55½
Africa	10,800,000	205,679,000	19
Oceanica	4,500,000	27,896,000	6
Total	48,800,000	1,479,706,500	170

These are estimated to speak 3,064 Languages, and possess about 1,000 different forms of Religion, with average duration of life, 33 years, classified in Races as follows: White Race, 616,000,000; Mongolian, 600,000,000; Black, 250,000,000; Copper Color, 12,000,000. There are 676,000,000 Pagans in religion; 320,000,000 Christians in Religion; 146,000,000 Mohammedans in Religion; 14,000,000 Jews in Religion.

WATER DIVISIONS.

	Square Miles.
Pacific	80,000,000
Atlantic	40,000,000
Indian	20,000,000
Southern	10,000,000
Arctic	5,000,000
Total	155,000,000

MANUFACTURER OF

THE LARGEST ASSORTMENT OF

Choice Chocolates

IN THE WORLD,

At 30c. Per Pound.

AREA AND POPULATION OF SOME OF THE PRINCIPAL COUNTRIES.

	Miles.	Population.
Chinese Empire	3,973,000	410,000,000
India	1,760,000	250,000,000
Russia, in Europe	2,092,000	76,500,000
United States, with Alaska	3,604,000	50,186,000
Germany	209,000	45,234,000
Austria	241,000	37,839,000
France	204,000	36,906,000
Great Britain and Ireland	121,000	34,862,000
Japan	150,000	34,338,000
Italy	114,000	28,452,000
Spain	196,000	16,623,000
Brazil	3,288,000	10,108,000
Mexico	742,000	9,637,000
Arabia	1,200,000	8,000,000
Persia	637,000	7,653,000
Sweden	172,000	4,567,000
British America	3,377,000	4,513,000
Argentine Confederation	1,100,000	2,400,000
Australia	3,120,000	2,197,000
Norway	122,000	1,807,000

A PUNCTUATION PUZZLE.

The following article forcibly illustrates the necessity of proper punctuation. It can be read in two ways, describing a very bad man or a very good man, the result depending upon the manner in which it is punctuated. It is very well worth the study of all, and particularly young printers.

He is an old and experienced man in vice and wickedness he is never found in opposing the works of iniquity he takes delight in the downfall of his neighbors he never rejoices in the prosperity of any of his fellow creatures he is always ready to assist in destroying the peace of society he takes no pleasure in serving the Lord he is uncommonly diligent in sowing discord among his friends and acquaintances he takes no pride in laboring to promote the cause of Christianity he has not been negligent in endeavoring to stigmatize all public teachers he makes no effort to subdue his evil passions he strives hard to build up Satan's kingdom he lends no aid to the support of the gospel among the heathen he contributes largely to the evil adversary he pays great heed to the devil he will never go to heaven he must go where he will receive the just recompense of reward.

COMPARATIVE HEIGHTS OF PRINCIPAL BUILDINGS IN THE WORLD.

Washington Monument	555 ft.
City Hall, Philadelphia,	537 " 4 in.
Cologne Cathedral,	510 "
Strasburg Cathedral,	468 "
St. Peter's, Rome,	448 "
St. Stephen's Cathedral, Vienna,	441 "
St. Rollox's Works, Glasgow,	430 "
Salisbury Cathedral, England,	404 "
Forazzo of Cremona,	396 "
Friburg Cathedral,	385 "
Amiens Cathedral, France,	383 "
Church of St. Peter, Hamburg,	380 "
The Cathedral, Florence,	376 "
Hotel de Ville, Brussels,	374 "
Tarre Asinelli, Bologna,	370 "
St. Paul's, London,	360 "
Church of St. Isaac, St. Petersburg,	336 "
Cathedral, Frankfort on Main,	326 "
Bell Tower, St. Marks, Venice,	323 "
Hotel des Invalides, Paris,	310 "
Boston Church, Lincolnshire, England,	292 "
U. S. Capitol, Washington,	287 "
Masonic Temple, Philadelphia,	280 "

AFTER HOURS CIGAR STORE.

Z. H. STREET,

DEALER IN

FINE DOMESTIC, KEY WEST, HAVANA AND IMPORTED CIGARS.

HEADQUARTERS FOR

After Hours and Espana High Grade Strictly Pure 5c. Cigars.

BOX TRADE A SPECIALTY.

328 CHESTNUT ST., PHILADELPHIA.

BOTTLING ESTABLISHMENT

OF

GUST. F. SCHOLLER,

215 N. FOURTH ST., PHILADELPHIA.

Sole Agent of Geo. Ehret's New York Lager Beer for the State of Pennsylvania.

FAMILIES SUPPLIED AT 75 CENTS PER DOZ.

GREAT ASSEMBLY ROOMS IN AMERICA & EUROPE,
HOLDING UPWARDS OF 2,000 PERSONS.

Building.	City.	Capacity
Colosseum	Rome	87,000
St. Peter's	Rome	58,000
Cathedral	Milan	40,000
Theatre of Pompey	Rome	40,000
St. Paul's	Rome	38,000
St. Paul's	London	31,000
St. Petronia	Bologna	26,000
Cathedral	Antwerp	25,000
Cathedral	Florence	23,000
St. John's Latern	Rome	23,000
St. Sophia's	Constantinople	23,000
Notre Dame	Paris	21,500
Theatre of Marcellus	Rome	20,000
Cathedral	Pisa	13,000
St. Stephen's	Vienna	12,400
St. Dominic's	Bologna	12,000
St. Peter's	Bologna	11,400
Cathedral	Vienna	11,000
Mormon Temple	Salt Lake City	10,000
Cathedral, Notre Dame	Montreal, Canada	10,000
St. Mark's	Venice	8,443
Gilmore's Garden	New York	7,500
Bolshoi Theatre	St. Petersburg	5,000
Music Hall	Cincinnati	4,824
Albert Hall	London	4,540
Grand Opera	Paris	4,350
La Scala Opera House	Milan	4,000
San Carlos	Naples	3,600
University Hall	Ann Arbor	3,500
Stadt Theatre	New York	3,105
Washington Hall	Paterson, N. J	3,000
City Hall	Columbus, O	3,000
Boston Theatre	Boston	2,972
Academy of Music	Philadelphia	2,805
Covent Garden Theatre	London	2,684
Music Hall	Boston	2,585
Carlo Felici	Genoa	2,560
Opera House	Birmingham, Pa	2,500
Music Hall	New Haven	2,500
Mobile Theatre	Mobile	2,500
Academy of Music	New York	2,433
Alexander	St. Petersburg	2,332
Opera House	Munich	2,307
Grand Opera House	Cincinnati	2,250
Haverly's Theatre	Chicago	2,238
Globe Theatre	Boston	2,200
St. Charles Theatre	New Orleans	2,178
Imperial	St. Petersburg	2,160
Academy of	Paris	2,092
Grand Opera Hall	New Orleans	2,052

LEADING RELIGIOUS DENOMINATIONS OF THE UNITED STATES, WITH SUNDAY SCHOOL ATTENDANCE.

	Attendance.	Sunday School Attendance.
Methodists	3,695,030	2,243,121
Baptists	2,471,448	1,127,090
Presbyterian	907,913	624,239
Lutheran	810,236	400,863
Congregationalists	382,000	168,976
Episcopal	362,000	206,463
Disciples of Christ	210,000	
Roman Catholic	6,000,000	468,124

IGNORANCE IN THE WORLD.

The percentage of illiteracy in the scale of 100 among the people of different countries is shown in the following table, taken from Kiddle and Scheme's "Cyclopædia of Education": India, 95; Mexico, 93; Poland, 91; Argentine Republic, 83; Greece, 82; Spain, 80; Italy, 73; Hungary, 51; China, 50; Austria, 49; Ireland, 46; England, 33; Belgium, 30; France, 30; United States, 20; Netherlands, 18; Scotland, 16; Japan, 10.

THE PETROLITE DISINFECTANT

The active disinfecting and cleansing powers of the **PETROLITE** have been recognized for years, but it was left for late chemical knowledge to so combine the materials in a harmless, clean and easily handled powder as to be convenient for use in our dwellings, or amongst clothing or textile fabrics.

PETROLITE DISINFECTANT

meets all these requirements, being **PENETRATING** and **POWERFUL** in its work, **CLEAN, HARMLESS** and **CONVENIENT** to handle. In its very **LOW COST** being adapted for use extensively in all places. It is also the sworn enemy of insects and vermin, which will not try to live where it is used. It is an unfailing remedy against Roaches, Moths, Bed-Bugs, and all kinds of insects.

This powder can be blown into crevices and cracks with the common insect gun. It can be used on **PLANTS, SHRUBS** and **FRUIT TREES.** Buy it and you will never be without.

As now is the time to guard our homes from impure and noxious vapors and smells, always generated at the warm season, creating disease, it will be the part of wisdom to try a can of

PETROLITE DISINFECTANT,

as it is an **UNFAILING DEODORIZER** for **WATER-CLOSETS, SINKS, CESSPOOLS**, etc , and **SURE PROTECTION** against **SEWER GAS.**

It is put up in neat tin cans, of one quart each, for 25 cents, or in larger packages for ten cents per pound.

MANUFACTURED BY

C. W. BILLMAN,

1903½ OXFORD ST., PHILADELPHIA, PA.

PLACES OF INTEREST IN PHILADELPHIA.

The City contains 35 Scientific Associations, 30 Public Libraries, 50 Religious Boards, 90 Charitable Associations, (dispensing nearly $2,000,000 per annum), 38 Hospitals, 25 Market-houses, 30 Public Cemeteries, 400 Churches, 26 Daily Papers and 45 Banks. There are 15 Theatres and Opera Houses open every evening, Sundays excepted.

The Gallery of Fine Arts, Academy of Music, Academy of Natural Sciences, and Zoological Garden are the largest on the Continent.

The new City Hall, when finished, will be one of the finest buildings of its kind in the world. It covers an area of 4½ acres; from North to South is 486 ft. 6 in.; East to West, 470 ft.; height of main tower, 537 ft., which will have a clock with a face 20 ft. in diameter. The building will contain 520 rooms. The figures on centre dormers are 17 ft. 6 in. in height; those on corner dormers 12 ft. 10 in. in height.

The Masonic Temple is the finest in the world, and is the greatest temple of the Masonic Order created since the Temple of Solomon. Its interior rooms are very beautiful. Open Thursdays. Free.

The New Post Office is a very fine building, situated at Ninth and Chestnut Streets.

The Mint. The Government has it in full operation. A collection of rare coins and medals is on exhibition. Open from 9 to 12 o'clock. Free. Daily.

The Library of Philadelphia (Locust and Juniper Streets). The foundation was laid in 1731 by Benjamin Franklin, and now contains 135,000 volumes.

The Ridgeway Branch Library, Broad and Carpenter Streets, is a gift from the late Dr. James Rush, son of Benjamin Rush. Building was occupied in 1870. Cost with grounds, $800,000. Will accommodate 400,000 books. It has been pronounced the finest in the world. The grand gallery contains the Loganian Library, 14,000 volumes, founded by James Logan 1750.

The University of Pennsylvania, founded 1760, comprises Six Departments, viz.: the Arts, Medicine, Law, Town's Scientific, Dentistry and Music. The Medical Department is acknowledged to be one of the best in the world. The Museum is unrivaled on this Continent.

Girard College, Twentieth and Girard Avenue. Open daily. Procure tickets at the *Ledger* Office. No charge. Take Ridge avenue or Nineteenth street cars. This is the finest specimen of Greek architecture in America. The view of Philadelphia from its marble roof is very fine and extended.

William Penn's House, in Fairmount Park is on Lansdowne Drive.

Independence Hall. Free. Open daily. Independence Square, Chestnut street between Fifth and Sixth. The Hall in which the Declaration of Independence was signed is on one side of the entrance, and a Museum of Relics of the Revolutionary period on the other. Open 9 A. M. to 4 P. M.

Academy of Fine Arts. Broad street above Arch street. Admission, 25 cents. This new and handsome edifice contains a very large collection of Paintings, Engravings, and Statuary. The School is the best in the country.

Pennsylvania Museum and School of Industrial Art. Exhibition in Memorial Art Building, Fairmount Park. The collection of objects of interest is the most unique in this country.

Young Men's Christian Association Building, Fifteenth and Chestnut Streets. This is a very beautiful building, and possesses many attractions.

Institution for the Blind, Race above Twentieth street (near Academy of Natural Sciences.)

Institution for the Deaf and Dumb, Broad and Pine streets.

Academy of Natural Sciences, Nineteenth and Race Streets. Over 250,000 specimens of Anatomical, Physical, and Natural Science. Its collection of Birds is not equaled. Open Tuesday and Friday afternoons. Admission, 15 cents.

Zoological Garden, Fairmount Park. Girard avenue cars. This collection and its beautiful grounds are not equaled in the United States.

Horticultural Garden, Fairmount Park, near Memorial Hall. Admission free. This beautiful Horticultural Building of Mauresque architecture, and the charming gardens, are a memorial of the Centennial. Weekly lectures, on Botany and Horticulture, are given on Saturdays.

Fairmount Park. This magnificent Park covers 3,000 acres. (Central Park, New York, has 843, and Druid Hill Park, Baltimore, 500 acres.) The beautiful Schuylkill flows through it for five miles, affording desirable facilities for boating and fishing, whilst its fine drives and lawns, its primitive and sylvan shades, its pleasant variety of hill and dale, its Palace of Industry, Zoological Garden, Memorial Hall, (with its treasures of Art,) and the Horticultural Hall, with its instructive display of rare plants, makes It the most delightful place of recreation in this country. In the Park are several fine monuments, of Lincoln, Witherspoon, Columbus, McMichael, and Meade, the Hebrew Monument to Religious Liberty, and the Catholic Monument to Temperance. The Fairmount Park Art Association have added many attractive Works of Art. At the east entrance is a very fine collection of Pompeian views. Visitors to the Park should not fail to see the enchanting Wissahickon Creek.

LARGE BRIDGES IN THE WORLD.

Niagara Suspension, 821 feet span. Allegheny, two spans, 344 feet each. The Covington and Cincinnati, one span of 1,057 feet. The Brooklyn and New York, one span of 1,595 feet. Railway bridge, now building over the Furth, Scotland, two spans, 1,680 feet each.

FOREIGN MONEYS AND THEIR VALUES IN UNITED STATES MONEY.

Country.	Monetary Unit.	Standard.	Value in U. S. Money
Austria	Florin	Silver	.40.6
Belgium	*Franc	Gold and Silver	.19.3
Bolivia	†Boliviano	Silver	.82.3
Brazil	Milreis of 1000 reis	Gold	.54.6
British America	Dollar	Gold	$1.00
Chili	Peso	Gold and Silver	.91.2
Cuba	Peso	Gold and Silver	.93.2
Denmark	§Crown	Gold	.26.8
Ecuador	†Peso	Silver	.82.3
Egypt	Piaster	Gold	.04.9
France	*Franc	Gold and Silver	.19.3
Great Britain	Pound sterling	Gold	4.86.6½
Greece	*Drachma	Gold and Silver	.19.3
German Empire	Mark	Gold	.23.8
Hayti	Gourde	Gold and Silver	.96.5
India	Rupee	Silver	.39
Italy	*Lira	Gold and Silver	.19.3
Japan	Yen	Silver	.88.7
Liberia	Dollar	Gold	1.00.
Mexico	Dollar	Silver	.89.4
Netherlands	Florin	Gold and Silver	.40.2
Norway	§Crown	Gold	.26.8
Peru	†Sol	Silver	.82.3
Portugal	Milreis	Gold	1.08
Russia	Rouble	Silver	.65.8
Sandwich Islands	Dollar	Gold	1.00
Spain	*Peseta	Gold and Silver	.19.3
Sweden	§Crown	Gold	.26.8
Switzerland	*Franc	Gold and Silver	.19.3
Tripoli	Mahbub	Silver	.74.3
Turkey	Piaster	Gold	.04.4
U. S. of Colombia	†Peso	Silver	.82.3
Venezuela	*Bolivar	Gold and Silver	.19.3

The above rates, proclamed by the Secretary of the Treasury, January 2, 1882, are used in estimating, for Custom House purposes, the values of all foreign merchandise made out in any of said currencies.

*The *franc* of France, Belgium, and Switzerland, the *peseta* of Spain, the *drachma* of Greece, the *lira* of Italy, and the *bolivar* of Venezuela, have the same value.

†The *peso* of Ecuador, and United States of Colombia, the *boliviano* of Bolivia, and the *sol* of Peru have the same value.

§The *crowns* of Norway, Sweden, and Denmark have the same value.

VALUE OF ANCIENT MONEY.

Denomination.	Grains.	Gold value.
Gold Shekel	132	$5.69
Gold Maneh	13,200	569.00
Gold Talent	1,132,000	56,900.00
Silver Gerah	11	.02¼
Silver Beka	110	.26½
Silver Shekel	220	.53
Silver Maneh	13,200	32.00
Silver Talent	660,000	1,660.00
Copper Shekel	528	.03 11/100
Persian Darie or Drachm (gold)	128	5.52
Maccabean Shekel (silver)	220	.53
"Piece of Money" (stater, silver)	220	.53
Penny (Denarius, silver)	58⅞	.14
Farthing (Quadrans, copper)	42	.00¼
Farthing (Assarium, copper)	84	.00½
Mite (copper)	21	.00⅛

THE SEVEN WONDERS OF THE WORLD.

The Egyptian Pyramids ; the Mausoleum, erected by Artemisia ; the Temple of Diana, at Ephesus ; the Walls and Hanging Gardens of Babylon ; the Colossus of Rhodes ; the Statue of Jupiter Olympus, and the Watch Tower at Alexandria.

ORIGINALITY, ECONOMY, EFFICIENCY

IN

ADVERTISING

IF ENTRUSTED TO

FREDERICK THOMAS,

WRITER, COMPILER AND SOLICITOR OF

"ATLANTIC CITY GUIDE," "THINGS YOU OUGHT TO KNOW,"

901 TASKER STREET, PHILADELPHIA,

OR AT THE PUBLISHERS,

BURK & McFETRIDGE, 306-308 CHESTNUT ST.

DISTANCES FROM PHILADELPHIA
— TO —

	Miles.		Miles.
Atlantic City, N. J.	59	Norristown, Pa.	17
Altoona, Pa.	237	New York City, N. Y	90
Albany, N. Y.	233	Newark, N. J.	80
Baltimore, Md.	98	New Brunswick, N. J	57
Boston, Mass.	320	Niagara Falls, N. Y	458
Bethlehem, Pa.	55	New Orleans, La.	1414
Bedford Springs, Pa	254	New Haven, Conn.	166
Bridgeton, N. J.	39	Newport, R. I.	256
Burlington, N. J.	19	Ocean Grove, N. J.	83
Chester, Pa.	14	Ogdensburg, N. Y.	484
Carlisle, Pa.	126	Omaha, Neb.	1320
Cape May, N. J.	81	Pittsburgh, Pa.	354
Cresson Springs, Pa	252	Pottstown, Pa.	40
Chambersburg, Pa.	157	Pottsville, Pa.	93
Chicago, Ill.	823	Portland, Me.	431
Cincinnati, O.	667	Quebec, Can	761
Cleveland, O.	504	Quincy, Ill.	1054
Charleston, S. C.	786	Reading, Pa	58
Columbus, Ohio	548	Rochester, N. Y.	377
Doylestown, Pa.	33	Richmond, Va.	254
Delaware Water Gap, N. J.	92	Sea Grove, N. J.	81
Downingtown, Pa	32	Salem, N. J.	44
Detroit, Mich.	683	San Francisco, Cal.	3220
Denver, Col.	1890	St. Joseph, Mo.	1337
Easton, Pa.	52	St. Louis, Mo.	1003
Erie, Pa.	446	Salt Lake City, Utah	2374
Elmira, N. Y.	283	St. Paul, Minn.	1274
Egg Harbor, N. J	42	Scranton, Pa.	163
Fort Wayne, Ind.	675	Savannah, Ga	767
Gettysburg, Pa.	135	Toledo, Ohio	615
Greensburg, Pa.	322	Trenton, N. J.	30
Harrisburg, Pa.	105	Tallahassee, Fla	1100
Huntingdon, Pa.	203	Uniontown, Pa.	360
Indianapolis, Ind.	722	Union City, Pa.	419
Ithaca, N. Y.	358	Utica, N. Y	326
Johnstown, Pa.	276	Valley Forge, Pa	23
Kansas City, Mo.	1277	Vineland, N. J.	34
Lancaster, Pa	72	Virginia City, Nev.	2784
Long Branch, N. J.	78	Williamsport, Pa.	198
Media, Pa.	13	Wilmington, Del.	28
Mauch Chunk, Pa.	89	Washington, D. C.	138
Mount Holly, N. J	29	Watkins Glen, N. Y.	299
Milwaukee, Wis.	863	Xenia, Ohio	603
Montgomery, Ala.	1037	York, Pa.	93
Montreal, Can.	589	Zanesville, O.	520

THE BIBLE.

The English version of the Bible contains: Old Testament, 2,728,100 letters, 592,439 words, 23,214 verses, 929 chapters, 39 books. The New Testament contains 838,380 letters, 181,253 words, 7,959 verses, 360 chapters, 27 books.

GREAT LIBRARIES.

Royal Library at Paris............................ ....824,000 volumes.
Bodleian Library at Oxford, Eng........................420,000 "
Royal Central Library, Munich...........................800,000 "
Vatican Library, Rome.......................... ....100,000 "
University Library, Gottingen...................... ....300,000 "
British Museum Library, London...... ....700,000 "
Library, Vienna.......... ....453,000 "
St. Petersburg Library, Russia.......... · ....505,000 "
Naples ....300,000 "
Dresden ....300,000 "
Copenhagen ....∴ ....557,000 "
Berlin ....460,000 "
Philadelphia Library.......................................135,000 "

Expansion and Contraction of Metals. The least is Glass, then as follows: Platinum, Steel, Iron, Gold, Copper, Brass, Silver, Tin, Lead, Zinc.

Best Conductors of Heat (Metals). Silver, Copper, Gold, Tin, Iron, Lead, Bismuth.

~ ESTABLISHED 1850 ~

TRADE · MARK.

PETER L. KRIDER,

MANUFACTURER OF

Sterling Silver Ware

GUARANTEED ${}^{925}_{1000}$ FINE.

Medal and Diploma Awarded at Centennial Exposition.

Striking Society Medals in Gold, Silver, Bronze and White Metal a Specialty.
Souvenir Medals by the 1,000 made to special order.

618 CHESTNUT STREET, PHILADELPHIA, PA.

CHARLES DICKENS ON "DEATH."

"Life like an empty dream flits by."

"Even when the golden hair lay in a halo on a pillow round the worn face of a little boy, he said with a radiant smile:—'Dear papa and mama, I am sorry to leave you both and to leave my pretty little sister, but I am called and I must go.' Thus the rustling of an angel's wings got blended with the other echoes, and had in them the breath of heaven."—*Tale of Two Cities, book 2, chapter* 21.

"There is no time there, and no trouble there. The spare hand does not tremble; nothing worse than a sweet, bright constancy is her face. She goes next before him—is gone."—*Ibid., book 2, chapter* 15.

"The dying boy made answer, 'I soon shall be there.' He spoke of beautiful gardens stretched out before him, that were filled with figures of men and many children, all with light upon their faces; then whispered it was Eden, and so died."—*Nicholas Nickleby, chapter* 58.

"'It's turned very dark, sir. Is there any light a-coming?' The cart is shaken all to pieces, and the rugged road is very near its end. I'm a-gropin'—a-gropin'—let me catch hold of your hand. Hallowed be thy name.'

"Dead! my lords and gentlemen. Dead! men and women, born with heavenly compassion in your hearts. And dying thus around us every day!"—*Bleak House, chapter* 47.

"He slowly laid his face down upon her bosom, drew his arm close round her neck, and with one parting sob began the world. Not this world. Oh, not this! The world that sets this right."—*Ibid., chapter* 65.

"'If this is sleep, sit by me when I sleep; turn me to you, for your face is going far off, and I want it to be near.' And she died like a child going to sleep."—*David Copperfield, chapter* 9.

"Time and the world were slipping from beneath him. He's going out with the tide. * * And it being low water he went out with the tide." *Ibid., chapter* 30.

"One new mound was there, which had not been there last night. Time, burrowing like a mole below the ground, had marked his track by throwing up another heap of earth."—*Martin Chuzzlewit, chapter* 16.

"She was dead. No sleep so beautiful and so calm, so free from trace of pain, so fair to look upon. She seemed a creature fresh from the hand of God and waiting for the breath of life, not one who had lived and suffered death. She was past all help or need of it. We will not wake her."—*Old Curiosity Shop, chapter* 71.

"The hand stopped in the midst of them; the light that had always been feeble and dim behind the weak transparency went out." *Hard Times, chapter* 9.

"For a moment the closed eyelids trembled and the faintest shadow of a smile was seen. Thus, clinging to the slight spar within her arms, the mother drifted out upon the dark and unknown sea that rolls around all the world."—*Dombey & Son, vol. 1, chapter* 1.

"It's very near the sea; I hear the waves! The light about the head is shining upon me as I go! The old, old fashion that came in with our first garments, and will last unchanged until our race has run its course and the wide firmament is rolled up like a scroll. Oh, thank God for that old fashion yet of immortality! And look upon us, angels of your children, when the swift river bears us to the ocean."—*Ibid., chapter* 17.

Atmospheric Pressure on the Human Frame is in all directions, and is rather more than 14½ lbs. per square inch, so that the average surface of an adult being 2,160 square inches, he has to bear an aggregate pressure of 31,536 lbs. It is calculated that the height of the atmosphere reaches 45 miles, where it entirely ceases.

WEIGHT AND STATURE OF MAN.

Mean weight, Males, 103.66 lbs.   Females, 93.73 lbs.

MALES.			FEMALES.		
Age—Years.	Feet.	Lbs.	Age—Years.	Feet.	Lbs.
0 "	1.64	7.06	0 "	1.62	6.42
2 "	2.60	25.01	2 "	2.56	23.53
4 "	3.04	31.38	4 "	3.00	28.67
6 "	3.44	38.80	6 "	3.38	35.29
9 "	4.00	49.95	9 "	3.92	47.10
11 "	4.36	59.77	11 "	4.26	56.57
13 "	4.72	75.81	13 "	4.60	72.65
15 "	5.07	96.40	15 "	4.92	89.04
17 "	5.36	116.56	17 "	5.10	104.34
18 "	5.44	127.59	18 "	5.13	112.55
20 "	5.49	132.46	20 "	5.16	115.30
30 "	5.52	140.38	30 "	5.18	119.82
40 "	5.52	140.42	40 "	5.18	121.81
50 "	5.49	139.96	50 "	5.04	123.86
60 "	5.38	136.07	60 "	4.97	119.76
70 "	5.32	131.27	70 "	4.97	113.60
80 "	5.29	127.54	80 "	4.94	108.80
90 "	5.29	127.54	90 "	4.94	108.81

❖SOMETHING CHOICE❖

Troth's Hams,

DELICIOUS ❖ FLAVOR.

ALL BRANDED

TROTH'S

WILLIAM J. TROTH,

1701, 1703, 1705 and 1707 SOUTH FOURTH ST.,

PHILADELPHIA, PA., U. S. A.

AUTHORS, POETS, AND HISTORIANS, AND THEIR EARNINGS.

Anthony Trollope. For twelve years his annual income from literature averaged £4,500, and in little over twenty years he made £70,000 by his pen. He made £727 in the aggregate by "The Warden" and "Barchester Towers," £250 for "The Three Clerks," £400 for "Dr. Thorne," £1,000 for "Framley Parsonage," and £3,500 for "Can You Forgive Her."

Mrs. Trollope received £800 for her work on "America," and it is believed for the next twenty years her literary income averaged £1,000 a year.

Mrs. Gore made a comfortable fortune out of her clever and interesting novels.

Miss Burney was paid £20 for "Evelina," £2,000 for "Cecilia," and £3,000 for "Camelia."

Miss Edgeworth. The highest sum this lady received for either of her Irish stories was £250.

George Eliot's total profit on "Remola" exceeded £10,000, and nearly double that sum on another of her works.

Wilkie Collins received £5,000 for "Armadale" before a line of it was written, and also £5,000 for "No Name."

Oliver Goldsmith received only £60 for his "Vicar of Wakefield."

Johnson was paid £100 for "Rasselus."

Dumas not only received nothing for his first novel, but had to pay for printing it, and although he made vast sums by his other works, the money was spent as soon as earned.

Lord Lytton is believed to have made over £80,000 by his novels.

Lord Beaconsfield is believed to have made quite £30,000 by his writings, although he profited but little by his earliest works.

Charles Dickens made as much by his readings as by his novels; his early bargains with publishers were deplorable, it is calculated that during the publishing of "Nicholas Nickleby" it appears that for three years previous he ought to have made £10,000 a year out of his writings. £7,000 was to have been paid him for "Edwin Drood," if he had lived to complete the twelve monthly parts.

Thackeray made most of his money by lecturing. He told a friend that he never made as much as £5,000 by any book he had written. Many of his works were not appreciated until after his death.

Sir Walter Scott's aggregate gains far exceeded any author that ever lived. He received £700 for "Waverley," and during the next nine years he received from his publisher £110,000. During the remaining eight years of his life he wrote eight more novels, as well as the "Life of Napoleon." For one of these novels he received £10,000, and £18,000 for "Life of Napoleon." Between November, 1825, and June, 1827, he received for his writings £26,000.

Tennyson (*Lord*), as a poet, has been by far the most successful in money getting.

Byron (*Lord*)   His total gain was only £23,000.

Thomas Moore.   The highest price paid him was £3,000 for his "Lalla Rookh."

Macaulay (*Lord*), as an Historian, ranks first-class.   His publishers undertook to pay him three-quarters of the net profits, and within a few months paid him £20,000 on account.

Goldsmith received £300 for "History of Rome," £250 for "History of Greece," and £600 for "History of England."

Gibbon gained £10,000 by the "Decline and Fall."

Thiers and Lamartine were each paid nearly £20,000 for their respective Histories.

Johnson was only paid £300 for "Lives of the Poets."

SWEET-MINDED WOMEN.

So great is the influence of a sweet-minded woman on those around her, that it is almost boundless.   It is to her that friends come in seasons of sickness and sorrow for help and comfort.   One soothing touch of her kindly hands works wonders in the feverish child ; a few words let fall from her lips in the ear of a sorrowing sister, do much to raise the load of grief that is bowing its victim down to the dust in anguish.   The husband comes home, worn out with the pressure of business, and feeling irritable with the world in general ; but when he enters the cosy sitting-room and sees the blaze of the bright fire, and meets his wife's smiling and happy face, he succumbs in a moment to the soothing influence.   We are all wearied with combating with the realities of life.   The rough schoolboy flies in a rage from the taunts of his companion to find solace in the mother's smile ; and so one may go on with instances of the influence a sweet minded woman has in the social life with which she is connected.   Beauty is an insignificant power when compared with hers.

Wheeler & Wilson's
NEW No. 8

The Lightest Running Two-thread Machine in the World.

NEW WOOD WORK.   NEW ATTACHMENTS.
VALUABLE IMPROVEMENTS.

AGENTS WANTED.

806 Chestnut Street, Philadelphia.

PRECIOUS STONES AND GOLD.

DIAMOND. ·The best are pure white like a drop of water, hence they are called of the firs: water. In some rare instances the color of a diamond, when not merely a tint, but of a decided hue, is an advantage as compared with those of the second water. Diamonds are pure carbon, like charcoal, and like it can be made to burn freely by elaborate chemical action. Diamonds are weighed with diamond carats, each of which is decimal 3¼ Troy grains.

SAPPHIRE is the hardest and most valuable of all gems except the diamond. It has a very remarkable effect to the eye, which can scarcely be described It occurs in many colors, of which Ruby is the most valuable, even more so than a diamond. The other colors most valued are blue, yellow and green, also called Emeralds. White Sapphires are often passed for diamonds. The finest yet discovered came from Ceyl n.

AMETHYST. A brilliant of a purplish violet color. The best are very valuable, but there is a common substance resembling them, only a species of quartz.

PEARLS The finest are found in a peculiar oyster, procured by divers from the bottom of the coast waters of the Indian Ocean. A good pearl resembles an opaque congealed tear of milk, with a bright surface. The largest and finest command fabulous prices, the value of which is teste l by weight in pearl grains, each pearl grain being ¼ of a Troy grain.

TOPAZ is a bright but not transparent stone, found in the tin mines of Bohemia and Saxony, in Brazil, and the Ural Mountains. It is of various colors,—red, green, blue, and yellow being the most usual.

GARNETS are of a blood red color, commonly called carbuncles. The best are from Ceylon and Greenland. Inferior stones, also called garnets, are found in many other places, varying in color, as red, yellow, green, and brown. There are black varieties called pyrenite; olive-green, called grossular; brown, called aplone, and yellow, called topazlite.

GOLD STANDARD. The fineness of gold is expressed in carats, the carat being the 24th part of the weight of the whole mass Thus the standard for gold coin in 21½ parts gold and 2½ parts alloy, that is 21½ carats. 18 carats has 3 parts gold and 1 part alloy, value 24 carat (Pure) Gold, $20.67 per oz. Standard Gold 21½ carat, $18.61 per oz. 18 carat, $15.50 per oz. 9 carat, $7 75 per oz.

GOLD, in the arts and manufactures, is valuable for its resistance to acids and the weather, and for its tenacity and malleability. So extreme is this, that a single grain of gold is capable of being drawn into 500 feet of wire, and of the finest gold leaf it takes the thickness of 28,000 leaves to make an inch. The only acid which will act in the least upon it is a mixture of muriatic and nitric. Pure gold will not lose a particle of weight by repeated melting. It assumes a greenish tinge when subjected to great heat. It is found minutely diffused in sandy quartz formations all over the world.

GREAT DOMES.

St. Paul's London	112 feet diam.,	215 feet high
Baths of Caracalla	112 "	" 116 " "
St. Sophia, Constantinople	115 "	" 201 " "
St. Peter's, Rome	139 "	" 330 " "
Duomo, Florence	139 "	" 310 " "
Reading Room at British Museum, London.	140 "	" 106 " "
Pantheon, Rome	142 "	" 143 " "

THE GREAT WALL OF CHINA.

It is 1250 miles long, 20 feet thick, and 20 feet high, with towers at short intervals from 30 to 40 feet high. It was built about 2000 years ago, and is said to have employed millions of men in its construction, and was completed in from five to ten years. It was built as a defence against their Northern enemies, the Tartars.

RELATIVE AGE OF ANIMALS.

The average age of a cat is 15 years; a bear, 20 years; a dog, 20 years; a wolf, 20 years; lions, up to 70 years; elephants, up to 400 years; a pig, to 20 years; rhinoceros, 20 years; horses average 28 years; camels, up to 100 years; stags are very long-lived; sheep seldom more than 10 years; cows, 15 years; it is considered probable that whales sometimes reach 1,000 years of age; eagles have lived to 104 years; ravens, 100; swans have been known to reach the age of 300 years, and tortoises to the age of 107 years.

BONAKER & JONES,

Makers of Fine Blank Books,

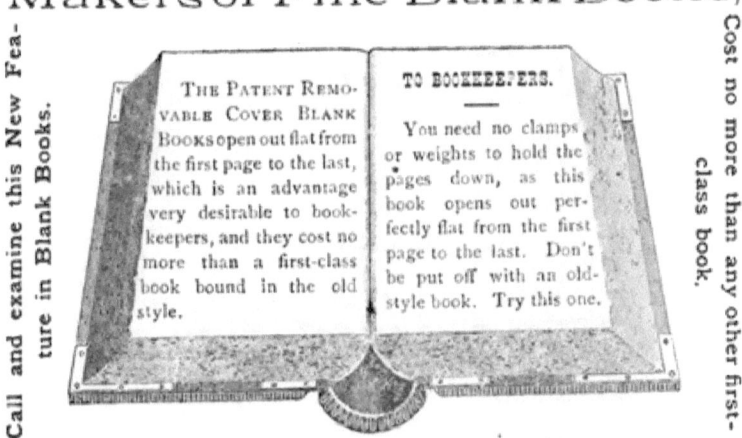

Call and examine this New Feature in Blank Books.

THE PATENT REMOVABLE COVER BLANK Books open out flat from the first page to the last, which is an advantage very desirable to bookkeepers, and they cost no more than a first-class book bound in the old style.

TO BOOKKEEPERS.

You need no clamps or weights to hold the pages down, as this book opens out perfectly flat from the first page to the last. Don't be put off with an old-style book. Try this one.

Cost no more than any other first-class book.

333 & 335 CHESTNUT STREET,

We bind books in the Old Style, which are far superior to any similar books in the market.

COMBINATION SHADES OF COLOR.

Red with Black..makes Brown.	
Lake with White.. " Rose.	
Amber with White.. " Drab.	
White with Brown... " Chestnut.	
Yellow with Brown.. " Chocolate.	
Red with Light Blue.. " Purple.	
Carmine with Straw... " Flesh color.	
Blue with Lead... " Pearl.	
Carmine with White... " Pink.	
Lamp Black with Indigo..................................... " Gray	
Black with White... " Lead.	
Paris Green with White..................................... " Bright Green.	
Yellow Ochre with White.................................... " Buff.	
Emerald Green with White................................... " Brill't Green.	
Vermilion with Chrome Yellow............................... " Orange.	
Chrome Yellow, Blue, Black and Red......................... " Olive.	
White with tints of Black and Purple....................... " Ash of Roses.	
White tinted with Purple................................... " French White.	

WEIGHTS AND MEASURES.

One quart of sifted flour is one pound.
One pint of granulated sugar is one pound.
Two cups of butter packed are one pound.
Ten eggs are one pound.
Five cupfuls of sifted flour are one pound.
A wineglassful is half a gill.
Eight even tablespoonfuls are a gill.
Four even saltspoonfuls make a teaspoonful.
A saltspoonful is a good measure of salt for all custards, puddings, blancmanges, &c.
One teaspoonful of soda to a quart of flour.
Two teaspoonfuls of soda to one of cream of tartar.
The teaspoonful given in all these receipts is just rounded full, not heaped.
Two heaping teaspoonfuls of baking powder to one quart of flour.
One cup of sweet or sour milk as wetting for one quart of flour.

CAPACITY OF BOXES.

The following table will be found exceedingly useful at times These are Inside dimensions :

A box 8⅜ in. by 8 in. and 8 in. deep, contains a peck.
A box 8 in. square and 4½ in. deep, contains a gallon
A box 7 in. square and 2¾ in. deep, contains a half gallon.
A box 4 in. square and 4½ in. deep, contains a quart.
A box 3 in. square and 3⅖ in. deep, contains a pint.
A box 24 in. by 17 in. and 28 in. deep, contains a barrel.
A box 18 in. by 15½ in. and 8 in. deep, contains a bushel.
A box 13½ in. square and 11¼ in. deep, contains a bushel.
A box 12 in. by 11½ in. and 9 in. deep, contains a half bushel.
A box 10 in. square and 10¾ in. deep, contains a half bushel.

RULES FOR DOSES OF MEDICINE SUITED TO DIFFERENT AGES.

If the dose for an adult is known, then for child
2 years old use about one-seventh.
4   "   "   one-fourth.
6   "   "   one-third.
8   "   "   one-half.
10   little over   "
15   "   two-thirds.
18   "   three-fourths.
21   full dose.

WEIGHTS AND MEASURES.
(Medicine.)

A drop is usually equal to a minim.
60 drops are equivalent to a teaspoonful or 1 drachm.
2 teaspoonsful or drachms equal to a dessertspoonful.
4 teaspoonfuls or drachms equal to 1 tablespoonful.
A wineglassful is 2 ounces or 4 tablespoonfuls.
A cupful is 4 ounces or 8 tablespoonfuls.
A tumblerful is 8 ounces or 16 tablespoonfuls.
60 grains—1 drachm.
480 grains—8 drachms or 1 ounce.
5760 grains—96 drachms or 12 ounces—1 pound, Troy.

ANTIDOTES FOR SOME OF THE MOST COMMON POISONS.

In giving directions for Antidotes, &c., for poisons taken by accident or through ignorance, it is impossible in this limited space to go into detail, and we shall only attempt to give some general directions to be employed while a physician is being sent for.

Emetics should be used first in almost all cases of poisoning, and should be given in divided doses until an effect is produced. The following are some of the best, and the quantities specified should *not* be given all at once, but as directed below :

Powdered Ipecac, 60 to 100 grains.
Sulphate Zinc, 30 grains.
Sulphate Copper, 15 grains.
Mustard, one or more tablespoonfuls.

Whichever is used, to be mixed with a tumblerful of warm water and given one-third at a time, every 5 or 10 minutes, till an effect is produced

RELATIVE DISTANCE OF DIFFERENT PLANETS FROM THE SUN.

	Miles.		Miles.
Vulcan	13,000,000,000	Earth	91,430,000
Neptune	2,745,998,000	Venus	66,134,000
Uranus	1,753,869,000	Mercury	35,392,000
Saturn	872.137,000	Earth's Moon from the	
Jupiter	475,692,000	Earth	230,800
Mars	139,311,000		

The following gives the diameter of the Sun, and the known principal planets that revolve around it, together with the number of moons belonging to the several planets.

Planets.	Diameter.	No. of Moons.	Planets.	Diameter.	No. of Moons.
Sun	852,900 miles		Venus	7,510 miles	
Jupiter	84,850 "	4	Mars	4,400 "	2
Saturn	70,150 "	8	Mercury	2.984 "	
Neptune	37,000 "	1	Earth	7,912 "	1
Uranus	33,000 "	6	Earth's Moon	2,165 "	

Daily revolution of each planet on its own axis.

Mars,	24 hours,	39 minutes,	2½ seconds.			
Mercury,	24 "	5 "	28 "			
Venus,	23 "	21 "	7 "			
Earth,	24 "					
Saturn,	10½ "					
Jupiter,	9 "	56 "				
Uranus,	7 "	5 "				

The Sun revolves around its own axis at the rate of 4,564 miles per hour.

The following is the time which the various planets require in moving around the sun.

Neptune	164¼ years.	Mars	1 yr. 10¼ mo.
Uranus	84 "	Earth	1 year.
Saturn	29½ "	Venus	224¾ days.
Jupiter	12 "	Mercury	88 "

The velocity with which the various planets move through space in revolving around the sun is as follows:

	Per Hour.		Per Hour.
Mercury	110,725 miles.	Saturn	22,309 miles.
Venus	80,000 "	Uranus	15,000 "
Earth	65,000 "	Neptune	12,000 "
Jupiter	30,000 "		

Our Moon makes a revolution around the earth in 28 days, hence called Lunar month, and gives heat to the surface of the earth 80,000th that of the sun, it has at its own surface 500 degrees of heat.

THE HUMAN BODY.

The average weight of the human body, in adult males, is 154 lbs., or 11 stone.

Elements of the human body are in the following proportions:

	lbs.	oz.	grs.
Oxygen, a gas	111	0	0
Carbon, a solid	21	0	0
Hydrogen, a gas	14	0	0
Nitrogen, a gas	3	9	0
Calcium, a solid	2	0	0
Phosphorus, a solid	1	12	190
Chlorine, a gas	0	2	382
Sulphur, a solid	0	2	219
Sodium, a metal	0	2	116
Fluorine, a gas	0	2	23
Potassium, a metal	0	0	290
Iron, a metal	0	0	100
Magnesium, a metal	0	0	12
Silicon, a non-metallic substance	6	0	12
	154	0	0

Compounds of the Human Body.—The elements of the body, in life, make compounds, of which the following are the proximate principles:

	lbs.	oz	grs.
Water	111	0	0
Gelatin, of which the skin and bones are principally composed	15	6	0
Fat	12	0	0
Phosphate of Lime	5	13	0
Fibrin, forming the muscles and the clot and globules of the blood	4	4	0
Albumen, found in the blood and nerves	4	3	0
Carbonate of Lime, also entering into the composition of bone	1	0	0
Chloride of Sodium, or common salt	0	3	376
Fluoride of Calcium, found in the bones	0	3	0
Sulphate of Soda	0	1	170
Carbonate of Soda	0	1	72
Phosphate of Soda	0	0	400
Sulphate of Potash	0	0	400
Peroxide of Iron	0	0	150
Phosphate of Potash	0	0	100
Phosphate of Magnesia	0	0	75
Chloride of Potassium	0	0	10
Silica	0	0	3
	154	0	0

Renewal of Human Bodies.—None of the constituents of the body remain permanently in the system, and whilst the old particles are being removed new ones are supplied by the food. It is calculated that a quantity of material, equal to the weight of the whole body, is carried away every forty days.

"CLEVELAND IS OUR PRESIDENT."

```
T N E D I S E R P R U O U R P R E S I D E N T
N E D I S E R P R U O S O U R P R E S I D E N
E D I S E R P R U O S I S O U R P R E S I D E
D I S E R P R U O S I D I S O U R P R E S I D
I S E R P R U O S I D N D I S O U R P R E S I
S E R P R U O S I D N A N D I S O U R P R E S
E R P R U O S I D N A L A N D I S O U R P R E
R P R U O S I D N A L E L A N D I S O U R P R
P R U O S I D N A L E V E L A N D I S O U R P
R U O S I D N A L E V E V E L A N D I S O U R
U O S I D N A L E V E L E V E L A N D I S O U

O S I D N A L E V E L C L E V E L A N D I S O

U O S I D N A L E V E L E V E L A N D I S O U
R U O S I D N A L E V E V E L A N D I S O U R
P R U O S I D N A L E V E L A N D I S O U R P
R P R U O S I D N A L E L A N D I S O U R P R
E R P R U O S I D N A L A N D I S O U R P R E
S E R P R U O S I D N A N D I S O U R P R E S
I S E R P R U O S I D N D I S O U R P R E S I
D I S E R P R U O S I D I S O U R P R E S I D
E D I S E R P R U O S I S O U R P R E S I D E
N E D I S E R P R U O S O U R P R E S I D E N
T N E D I S E R P R U O U R P R E S I D E N T
```

The above can be read upward of five thousand different ways, by starting with the centre letter C and taking the most zigzag course to any of the four corners, viz.:—"Cleveland is our President."

A WOMAN'S CHANCES OF MARRIAGE AT VARIOUS AGES.

This curiously constructed exhibit, by Dr. Granville, is drawn up from the registered cases of 876 married women in France. Owing to the difference in our climate, it will be safe to say that French women are as mature at 18 as American women at 20. Of the 876 tabulated, there were married :

Marriages.		Years of Age.	Marriages.		Years of Age.
3	at	13	28	at	27
11	at	14	22	at	28
16	at	15	17	at	29
43	at	16	9	at	30
45	at	17	8	at	31
77	at	18	5	at	32
115	at	19	7	at	33
118	at	20	5	at	34
86	at	21	3	at	35
85	at	22	0	at	36
59	at	23	2	at	37
53	at	24	0	at	38
36	at	25	1	at	39
24	at	26	0	at	40

A careful examination of statistics has demonstrated that the best results would follow if our girls did not marry until at least 20 years of age, and our men until they were 25.

Dr. C. A. White's

Celebrated Sets of Teeth,
from $5 to $40.
Fillings, $1.

826 Arch St., Philada.

HOW TO PREVENT FIRES.

1. Always buy the best quality of oil.

2. Never make a sudden motion with a lamp, either in lifting it or setting it down.

3. Never place a lamp on the edge of a table or mantel.

4. Never fill a lamp after dark, even if you should have to go without a light.

5. See that the lamp wicks are always clean and that they work freely in the tube.

6. Never blow out a lamp from the top.

7. Never take a light to a closet, where there are clothes. If necessary to go to the closet, place the light at a distance.

8. Use candles just as much as possible in going about the house, and in bed rooms. They are cheaper, can't explode, and for very many purposes just as good as lamps.

9. Matches should always be kept in stone or earthen jars or in tin.

10. They should never be left where rats or mice can get hold of them. There is nothing more to the taste of a rat than phosphorus. They will eat it if they can get at it. A bunch of matches is almost certain to be set on fire if a rat gets at it.

11. Have perfectly good safes in every place where matches are to be used, and never let a match be left on the floor.

12. Never let a match go out of your hand after lighting it until you are sure the fire is out, and then it is better to put it in a stove or an earthen dish.

13. It is far better to use the safety match, which can only be lighted upon the box which contains them.

14. Have your furnaces examined carefully in the fall and at least once during the winter by a competent person. All of the pipes and flues should be carefully looked to.

15. If there are any closets in the house near chimneys or flues, which there ought not to be, put nothing of a combustible nature into them. Such closets will soil silver and crack crockery, and burn bedding. They form a bad part of any home that contains them.

16. Never leave any wood near a furnace, range or stove to dry.

17. Have your stoves looked to frequently to see that there are no holes for coal to drop out.

18. Never put any hot ashes or coal in a wooden receptacle.

19. Be sure there are no curtains or shades that can be blown into a gaslight.

20. Never examine a gas meter after dark.

HOW FAST WILD DUCKS FLY.

The canvas-back can distance the whole duck family. When the canvas-back is out taking things easy, it jogs through the air at the rate of eighty miles an hour. If it has business somewhere and has to get there it puts two miles behind it every minute.

The mallard duck is a slow coach. It's all he wants to do to go a mile a minute, but he can do it when it is necessary. His ordinary, every-day style of getting along over the country gets him from place to place about a 45-mile-an-hour rate.

The black duck is about an even mate for the mallard, and the pin-tail widgeon and wood duck can't do much better.

The redhead can sail along with ease and cover his ninety miles an hour as long as he feels inclined to.

The blue-winged teal and its handsome cousin, the green-winged teal, could fly side by side for a hundred miles and make the distance neck and neck, for one can fly just as fast as the other, and to go one hundred miles an hour is no hard task for either of them.

AMONG the "curiosities of commerce" none perhaps, is more curious than that the major portion of the produce exported from South Africa is simply used for the adornment of ladies. Out of a total value exported of £7,500,000, ostrich feathers and diamonds account for £5,000,000.

FROM Kimberley, South Africa, a mining oasis in an agricultural district, has been sent, in the last fifteen years, something like £40,-000,000 worth of diamonds in the rough, which, with the cost of cutting, setting and selling must have taken from the pockets of consumers something approaching £100,000,000.

THE ENGLISH BILLION.

The English billion—a million millions—has set Sir Henry Besse-mer to calculating. He reckons that a billion seconds have not elapsed since the world began, as they would reckon 31,687 years, 17 days, 22 hours, 45 minutes, 5 seconds. A chain of a billion sovereigns would pass 736 times around the globe, or lying side by side, each in contact with its neighbor, would form about the earth a golden zone 26 feet 6 inches wide. This same chain, were it stretched out straight, would make a line a fraction over 18,328,455 miles in extent. For measuring height, Sir Henry chose for a unit a single sheet of paper of about one three hundred and thirty-third of an inch in thickness. A billion of these thin sheets, pressed out flat and piled vertically upon each other, would attain an altitude of 47,348 miles.

OXYGEN AND HUMAN LIFE.

At every moment of his life man is taking oxygen into his system by means of the organs of respiration. The body of an adult man, supplied with sufficient food, has neither increased nor diminished in weight at the end of twenty-four hours; yet the quantity of oxygen taken into the system during this period is very considerable, amounting in a year to from 700 to 800 lbs. This oxygen is given off from the lungs in combination with carbonic acid gas and hydrogen in the form of vapor.

THE SUN DIAL.

The date of the invention of the sun dial is unknown, but the earliest mention of it is in the Bible, in the Second Chronicles, thirty-second chapter, twenty-fourth verse, where it is recorded that Hezekiah was sick and prayed unto the Lord, and received in answer a sign, which is particularly described in Isaiah, thirty-eighth chapter, eighth verse, as follows:—"Behold, I will bring again the shadow of the degrees which is gone down in the sun dial of Ahaz ten degrees backward. So the sun returned ten degrees, by which degrees it was gone down." Seven hundred years before the Christian era the Chaldeans, among the earliest astronomers, divided the day into sixty parts in some manner, but the first sun dial used by them was the hemicycle or hemisphere made by Berosus, who lived about 540 B. C.

PERCENTAGE OF NUTRITION IN VARIOUS ARTICLES OF FOOD.

Raw Cucumbers	2	Raw Beef	26
Raw Melons	3	Raw Grapes	27
Boiled Turnips	4½	Raw Plums	29
Milk	7	Broiled Mutton	30
Cabbage	7½	Oatmeal Porridge	75
Currants	10	Rye Bread	79
Whipped Eggs	13	Boiled Beans	87
Beets	14	Boiled Rice	88
Apples	16	Barley Bread	88
Peaches	20	Wheat Bread	90
Boiled Codfish	21	Baked Corn Bread	91
Broiled Venison	22	Boiled Barley	92
Potatoes	22½	Butter	93
Fried Veal	24	Boiled Peas	93
Roast Pork	24	Raw Oils	94
Roast Poultry	26		

WAGES TABLE.

SALARIES AND WAGES BY THE YEAR, MONTH, WEEK OR DAY, SHOWING
WHAT ANY SUM FROM $20 TO $1600 PER ANNUM,
IS PER MONTH, WEEK OR DAY.

Per Year	Per Month	Per Week	Per Day	Per Year	Per Month	Per Week	Per Day
$20 is	$1.67	$0.38	$0.05	$280 is	$23.33	$5.37	$0.77
25	2.08	.48	.07	285	23.75	5.47	.78
30	2.50	.58	.08	290	24.17	5.56	.79
35	2.92	.67	.10	295	24.58	5.66	.81
40	3.33	.77	.11	300	25.00	5.75	.82
45	3.75	.86	.12	310	25.83	5.95	.85
50	4.17	.96	.14	320	26.67	6.14	.88
55	4.58	1.06	.15	325	27.08	6.23	.89
60	5.00	1.15	.16	330	27.50	6.33	.90
65	5.42	1.25	.18	340	28.33	6.52	.93
70	5.83	1.34	.19	350	29.17	6.71	.96
75	6.25	1.44	.21	360	30.00	6.90	.99
80	6.67	1.53	.22	370	30.83	7.10	1.01
85	7.08	1.63	.23	375	31.25	7.19	1.03
90	7.50	1.73	.25	380	31.67	7.29	1.04
95	7.92	1.82	.26	390	32.50	7.48	1.07
100	8.33	1.92	.27	400	33.33	7.67	1.10
105	8.75	2.01	.29	425	35.42	8.15	1.16
110	9.17	2.11	.30	450	37.50	8.63	1.25
115	9.58	2.21	.32	475	39.58	9.11	1.30
120	10.00	2.30	.33	500	41.67	9.59	1.37
125	10.42	2.40	.34	525	43.75	10.07	1.44
130	10.83	2.49	.36	550	45.83	10.55	1.51
135	11.25	2.59	.37	575	47.92	11.03	1.58
140	11.67	2.69	.38	600	50.00	11.51	1.64
145	12.08	2.78	.40	625	52.08	11.99	1.71
150	12.50	2.88	.41	650	54.17	12.47	1.78
155	12.92	2.97	.42	675	56.25	12.95	1.85
160	13.33	3.07	.44	700	58.33	13.42	1.92
165	13.75	3.16	.45	725	60.42	13.90	1.99
170	14.17	3.26	.47	750	62.50	14.38	2.05
175	14.58	3.36	.48	775	64.58	14.86	2.12
180	15.00	3.45	.49	800	66.67	15.34	2.19
185	15.42	3.55	.51	825	68.75	15.82	2.26
190	15.83	3.64	.52	850	70.83	16.30	2.33
195	16.25	3.74	.53	875	72.92	16.78	2.40
200	16.67	3.84	.55	900	75.00	17.26	2.47
205	17.08	3.93	.56	925	77.08	17.74	2.53
210	17.50	4.03	.58	950	79.17	18.22	2.60
215	17.92	4.12	.59	975	81.25	18.70	2.67
220	18.33	4.22	.60	1000	83.33	19.18	2.74
225	18.75	4.31	.62	1050	87.50	20.14	2.88
230	19.17	4.41	.63	1100	91.67	21.10	3.01
235	19.58	4.51	.64	1150	95.83	22.06	3.15
240	20.00	4.60	.66	1200	100.00	23.01	3.29
245	20.42	4.70	.67	1250	104.17	23.29	3.42
250	20.83	4.79	.69	1300	108.33	24.93	3.56
255	21.25	4.89	.70	1350	112.50	25.89	3.70
260	21.67	4.99	.71	1400	116.67	26.85	3.84
265	22.08	5.08	.73	1450	120.84	27.80	3.98
270	22.50	5.18	.74	1500	125.00	28.77	4.11
275	22.92	5.27	.75	1600	133.34	30.68	4.38

AMERICAN GEOGRAPHICAL NAMES, WITH THEIR DERIVATION AND SIGNIFICATION.

ALBANY, awl'ba-ne, N. Y., named in honor of the Duke of York and Albany, afterward James II., at the time it came into possession of the English, in 1664.

ALLEGHANY, al'le-gā-ne (Ind.), river of the Alligewi.

AMERICA, a-mer'e-kah, named after Amerigo Vespucci, who in 1497 landed upon the continent south of the equator.

ARIZONA, ar-e-zo'nah, sand hills.

ARKANSAS, ar-kan'sas, formerly and erroneously pronounced ar-kan-saw, from Ka. sas, with the French prefix, of arc, a bow.

BALTIMORE, bawl-te-mōr, named after Lord Baltimore, who settled the province of Maryland, in 1635.

BEHRING'S STRAITS, beer'ingz strätz, named by Captain Cook after Behring, their discoverer.

BERMUDAS, ber-mū'daz, named after Juan Bermudez, their Spanish discoverer.

BOSTON, bos'tn, originally St. Botolph's town.

BRAZIL, bra-zil' Portuguese pron. Bra-zeel, from the Spanish or Portuguese name of the dye-wood exported from the country.

CALIFORNIA, kal-e-for'ne-ah, a name given by Cortes, in the year 1535, to the peninsula now called Lower or Old California, of whi. h he was the discoverer.

CANADA, kan'a-dah (Ind.), a collection of huts; a village; a town.

CATSKILL, katz'kil (D. Katzkill), mountains, so called from the panthers or lynxes which formerly infested them.

CAROLINA, kar-o-li'nah, named after Charles I., of England.

CHARLESTON, charls'tn, S. C., named after Charles I., of England.

CHESAPEAKE, ches'a-peek (Ind.), great waters.

CHICAGO, she-kaw'go, a French form of an Indian word signifying a skunk; also, a wild onion, from its strong and disagreeable odor.

CHILI, chil'le, (Peruv.), land of snow.

COLORADO, kol-o-rah'do (Sp.), red or colored.

COLUMBIA, ko-lum'be-ah, named after Christopher Columbus.

CONNECTICUT, kon-net'e-kut (Ind. Qunni-tuk-ut, (the country) "upon the long river."

DELAWARE, del-a-wāre, named in honor of Thomas West, Lord de la Ware, who visited the bay in 1610, and died on his vessel, at its mouth.

DETROIT, de-troit,' (Fr.), named from the river or "strait" (Fr. detroit) on which it is built.

FLORIDA, flor'e-dah, named by Ponce de Leon from the day on which he discovered it, Easter Sunday, called in Spanish, Pasqua Florida.

GEORGIA, geor'ge-ah, named in honor of George II., of England.

HUDSON, hud'sn, named after Henry Hudson, who ascended the river in 1607.

INDIANA, in'de-an''ah, from the word Indian.

ILLINOIS, il-le-noiz' or il-le-noi, from Ind. illini, men, and the French suffix ois, "tribe of men."

IOWA, i'o-wah, the French form of the Indian word, signifying "the drowsy," or the "sleepy ones;" a Sioux name of the Pahoja or "Gray-snow" tribe.

JAMAICA, ja-ma'kah (Ind. Cay-may-ca, or Kay-may-ca), said to mean "a country abounding in springs."

KANSAS, kan'sas (Ind.), smoky water; also said to signify good potato

KENTUCKY, ken-tuk'e (Ind.), at head of a river.

LOUISIANA, loo'e-ze-ah''nah, named after Louis XIV., of France.

MANHATTAN, man-hat'tn (Ind. munnoh-atan), the town on the island.

MARYLAND, ma're-land, named after Henrietta Maria, queen of Charles I.

MASSACHUSETTS, mas'sa-chu''sets (Ind.), about the great hills; *i. e.*, the "Blue Hills."

MEMPHIS, mem'fis, the temple of the Good God.

MILWAUKEE, mil-waw'ke (Ind.), rich land.

MINNESOTA, min-ne-so'tah (Ind.), cloudy water ; whitish water.

MISSISSIPPI, mis-sis-sip'pi (Ind.), great and long river.

MISSOURI, mis-soo're (Ind.), muddy.

MOHAWK, mo'hawk (Ind.), man-eaters. Literally, it signifies eaters of live food, a name given by the New England or Eastern Indians to the Iroquois.

NEBRASKA, ne-bras'kah (Ind.), water valley ; shallow river.

NEWFOUNDLAND, nu-fund-land, named by its discoverer, John Cabot, in 1497, first applied to all the territory discovered by him, but afterward restricted to the island to which it is now applied.

NEW HAMPSHIRE, nu-hamp'sheer, named after the county of Hampshire in England.

NEW JERSEY, nu-jer'ze, named in honor of Sir James Carteret, an inhabitant of the isle of Jersey.

NEW YORK, nu york, named after the Duke of York, afterwards James II.

NIAGARA, ni-ag'a-rah (Ind.), neck of water ; connecting Lake Erie with Lake Ontario.

NOVA SCOTIA, no'va-sko'she-ah (Lat.), New Scotland.

OHIO, o-hi'o (Ind.), beautiful.

ONTARIO, on-te're-o (Ind.), from Onontee, "a village on a mountain," the chief seat of the Onondagas.

OREGON, or'e-gn, named by Carver Oregon or Oregan ; *i. e.*, River of the West.

OTTAWA, ot-tah'wah (Ind.), traders.

PENNSYLVANIA, pen'sil-va''ne-ah, Penn's woods (Lat. Sylva, a wood), named after William Penn, who settled the country in 1681.

PHILADELPHIA, fil-a-del'fe-ah (Gr.), a city of brotherly love.

QUEBEC, kwe-bek', an Algonquin term, meaning "take care of the rock."

RHODE ISLAND, rode i'land, named from a fancied resemblance to the island of Rhodes.

SAN DOMINGO, san do-ming'go (Sp.), Holy Sabbath.

SAN FRANCISCO, san fran-sis'ko (Sp.), St. Francis.

SANTA CRUZ, san'tah croos, (Sp.), Holy Cross.

SANTA FE, san-tah fa (Sp.), Holy Faith.

TENNESSEE, ten-nes-see' (Ind.), river of the Big Bend.

TIOGA, ti-o'gah (Ind.) swift current.

TOLEDO, to-le'do (Lat. Toledum), named by its Jewish founders from Heb. toledoth, generations, families, races.

TORONTO, to-ron'to (Ind.), an Iroquois term denoting oak trees rising from the lake.

VERMONT, ver-mont', from Fr. verb, green ; mont, mountain ; green mountains.

VIRGINIA, vir-gin'e-ah, named in honor of Queen Elizabeth, the Virgin Queen, in whose reign Sir Walter Raleigh made the first attempt to colonize this region.

WASHINGTON, wosh'ing-tun, named after George Washington, the first president of the United States.

WINNIPEG, win'ne-peg (Ind.), turbid water.

WISCONSIN, wis-kon'sin, wild rushing channel.

AIR-LINE DISTANCES FROM WASHINGTON TO VARIOUS PARTS OF THE WORLD.

	Miles.		Miles.
Alexandria, Egypt	5,275	Manilla, Phil. Islands	9,360
Amsterdam, Holland	3,555	Mecca, Arabia	6,598
Athens, Greece	5,005	Muscat, Arabia	7,600
Auckland, N. Z	8,290	Monrovia, Liberia	3,645
Algiers, Algeria	3,425	Morocco, Morocco	3,305
Berlin, Prussia	3,847	Mourzouk, Fezzan	5,525
Berne, Switzerland	3,730	Mozambique, Moz.	7,348
Brussels, Belgium	3,515	Ottawa, Canada	462
Batavia, Java	11,118	Panama, New Gran.	1,825
Bombay, Hindoostan	8,548	Parana, A. C	4,733
Buenos Ayres, A. C	5,013	Port au Prince, Hayti	1,425
Bremen, Prussia	3,500	Paris, France	3,485
Constantinople, Turkey	4,880	Pekin, China	8,783
Copenhagen, Denmark	3,895	Quebec, Canada	601
Calcutta, Hindostan	9,348	Quito, Ecuador	2,531
Canton, China	9,000	Rio Janeiro, Brazil	4,280
Cairo, Egypt	5,848	Rome, Italy	4,365
Cape Town, Cape Colony	6,684	St. Petersburg, Russia	4,296
Cape of Good Hope	7,380	Stockholm, Sweden	4,055
Caraccas, Venezuela	1,805	Shanghai, China	8,600
Charlotte Town, P. E. I	820	Singapore, Malay	11,300
Dublin, Ireland	3,076	St. John's, N. F	1,340
Delhi, Hindostan	8,368	San Domingo, S. D	4,300
Edinburgh, Scotland	3,275	San Juan, Nicaragua	1,740
Frederickton, N. B	670	San Salvador, A. C	1,650
Gibralter, Spain	3,150	Santiago, Chili	4,970
Glasgow, Scotland	3,215	Spanish Town, Jamaica	1,446
Halifax, N. S.	780	Sydney, C. B. I	975
Hamburg, Germany	3,570	Sydney, Australia	8,963
Havana, Cuba	1,139	St. Paul de Loanda	5,578
Honolulu, S. I	4,513	Timbuctoo, Soudan	3,395
Jerusalem, Palestine	5,495	Tripoli, Tripoli	4,425
Jamestown, St. Helena	7,150	Tunis, Tunis	4,240
Lima, Peru	3,515	Toronto, Canada	343
Lisbon, Portugal	3,190	Venice, Italy	3,835
Liverpool, England	3,228	Vienna, Austria	4,115
London, England	3,315	Valparaiso, Chili	4,934
City of Mexico, Mex	1,867	Vera Cruz, Mexico	1,680
Montevideo, Uruguay	5,003	Warsaw, Poland	4,010
Montreal, Canada	471	Yeddo, Japan	7,630
Madrid, Spain	3,485	Zanzibar, Zanzibar	7,078
Moscow, Russia	4,466		

PRESIDENTS OF THE UNITED STATES OF AMERICA.

	Born.	Inaugurated.	Died.	Native of.
George Washington	Feb. 22, 1732	April 30, 1789	Dec. 14, 1799	Virginia.
John Adams	Oct. 30, 1735	March 4, 1797	July 4, 1826	Massachusetts.
Thomas Jefferson	April 2, 1743	March 4, 1801	July 4, 1826	Virginia.
James Madison	March 16, 1751	March 4, 1809	June 28, 1836	Virginia.
James Monroe	April 2, 1759	March 4, 1817	July 4, 1831	Virginia.
John Quincy Adams	July 11, 1767	March 4, 1825	Feb. 23, 1848	Massachusetts.
Andrew Jackson	March 15, 1767	March 4, 1829	June 8, 1845	South Carolina.
Martin Van Buren	Dec. 5, 1782	March 4, 1837	July 25, 1862	New York.
*William Henry Harrison	Feb. 9, 1773	March 4, 1841	April 4, 1841	Virginia.
John Tyler	March 29, 1790	April 5, 1841	Jan. 17, 1862	Virginia.
James K. Polk	Nov. 2, 1795	March 4, 1845	June 15, 1849	North Carolina.
Zachary Taylor	Nov. 24, 1790	March 4, 1849	July 9, 1850	Virginia.
*Millard Fillmore	Jan. 7, 1800	July 10, 1850	March 8, 1874	New York.
Franklin Pierce	Nov. 23, 1804	March 4, 1853	Oct. 8, 1869	New Hampshire.
James Buchanan	April 23, 1791	March 4, 1857	June 1, 1868	Pennsylvania.
*Abraham Lincoln	Feb. 12, 1809	March 4, 1861	April 15, 1865	Kentucky.
*Andrew Johnson	Dec. 29, 1808	April 15, 1865	July 31, 1875	North Carolina.
Ulysses S. Grant	April 27, 1822	March 4, 1869		Ohio.
Rutherford B. Hayes	Oct. 4, 1822	March 5, 1877		Ohio.
*James A. Garfield	Nov. 19, 1831	March 4, 1881	Sept. 19, 1881	Ohio.
*Chester A. Arthur	Oct. 5, 1830	Sept. 19, 1881		Vermont.
Grover Cleveland	March 18, 1837	March 4, 1885		New Jersey.

* Elected Vice-Presidents, and succeeded to the Presidency upon the death of the President.

HIGHEST MOUNTAINS IN THE WORLD,

WITH HEIGHT IN FEET AND MILES.

	Feet.	*Miles.*
unchainyunga, Himalayas	28,178	5⅓
rata, Andes, highest in America	25,380	5
limani, Bolivia	21,780	4⅛
himborazo, Ecuador	21,444	4⅛
indoo-Koosh, Afghanistan	20,600	3¾
otopaxi, Ecuador	19,408	3⅔
ntisana, Ecuador	19,150	3½
. Elias, British America	18,000	3⅓
opocatapetl Volcano, Mexico	17,735	3⅜
t. Roa, Hawaii	16,000	3
t. Brown, highest Rocky Mountain peak	15,900	3
ont Blanc, highest in Europe	15,776	3
owna Roas, Owhyhee	15,700	3
ount Rosa, Alps, Sardinia	15,550	3
inchinca, Ecuador	15,200	2⅞
t. Whitney, Cal	15,000	2¾
ount Fairweather, Russian Possessions.	14,796	2¾
ount Shasta, California	14,450	2¾
ike's Peak, Colorado	14,320	2¾
ount Ophir, Sumatra	13,800	2⅝
remont's Peak, R. M., Wyoming	13,570	2⅝
ong's Peak, R. M., California	13,400	2½
ount Ranier, Washington Territory	13,000	2½
ount Ararat, Armenia	12,700	2⅜
eak of Teneriffe, Canaries	12,236	2¼
iltsin, Morocco	12,000	2¼
ount Hood, Oregon	11,570	2¼
implon, Alps	11,542	2¼
ount Lebanon, Syria.	11,000	2⅛
ount Perdu, France	10,950	2
ount St. Helen's, Oregon	10,158	1⅞
ount Etna, Sicily	10,050	1⅞
lympus, Greece	9,754	1¾
t. Gothard, Alps	9,080	1¾
ilate, Alps	9,050	1¾
ount Sinai, Arabia	8,000	1½
indus, Greece	7,677	1½
lack Mountain, New Caledonia	6,467	1¼
ount Washington, New Hampshire	6,234	1¼
ount Marcy, New York	5,467	1
ount Hecla, Iceland	5,000	1
en Nevis, Scotland	4,400	¾
ansfield, Vermont	4,280	¾
eaks of Otter, Virginia.	4,260	¾
en Lawers, Scotland	4,030	¾
arnassus, Greece	3,950	¾
esuvius, Naples	3,932	¾

SCRIPTURAL MEASURES OF LENGTH,

WITH ENGLISH EQUIVALENTS.

The great Cubit was 21.888 ins.=1.824 ft., and the less 18 ins. A span the longer=½ a cubit=10.944 ins.=.912 ft. A span the less=¼ of a cubit=7.296 ins.=.608 ft. A hand's breadth=1-6 of a cubit=3.684 ins.=.304 ft. A finger's breadth=1.24 of a cubit=.912 ins.=.076 ft. A fathom=4 cubits=7.296 ft. *Ezekiel's* Reed=6 cubits=10.944 ft. The mile=4,000 cubits=7,196 ft. The Stadium, 1-10 of their mile=400 cubits=729.6 ft. The Parasang, 3 of their miles=12,000 cubits, or 4 English miles and 580 ft. 33.164 miles was a day's journey—some say 24 miles; and 3,500 ft. a Sabbath day's journey; some authorities say 3,648 ft.

SCRIPTURAL MEASURES OF CAPACITY,

WITH ENGLISH EQUIVALENTS.

The Chomer or Homer in King James's translation was 75.625 gals. liquid, and 32.125 pecks dry. The Ephah or Bath was 7 gals., 4 pts., 15 ins. sol. The Seah, ⅓ of Ephah, 2 gals., 4 pts., 3 in. sol. The Hin=1-6 of Ephah, 1 gal., 2 pts., 1 in. sol. The Omer=1-10 of Ephah, 5 pts., 0.5 ins. sol. The Cab=1-18 of Ephah, 5 pts.; 10 ins. sol. The Log=7 1-72 of Ephah, ½ pt., 10 ins. sol. The metretes of *Syria* (*John* ii, 6)=Cong. Rom. 7¼ pts. Cotyla Eastern=1-100 of Ephah, ¼ pt., 3 in. sol. This Cotyla contains just 10 ozs. Avordupois of rain water. Omer, 100; Ephah, 1,000; Chomer or Homer, 10,000.

LIMIT OF PERPETUAL SNOW,

AND GROWTH OF TREES.

On the Andes, in lat. 2 deg., the limit of perpetual snow is 14,760 ft. In Mexico, lat. 19 deg., the limit is 13,800 ft.; on the peak of Teneriffe, 11,454 ft.; on Mount Etna, 9,000 ft.; on Caucasus, 9,900 ft. on the Pyrenees, 8,400 ft.; in Lapland, 3,100 ft.; in Iceland, 2,890 ft. The walnut ceases to grow at an elevation of 3,600 ft.; the yellow pine at 6,200 ft.; the ash at 4,800 ft.; and the fir at 6,700 ft. The loftiest inhabited spot on the globe is the Port House of Ancomarca, on the Andes, in Peru, 16,000 feet above the level of the sea. The 14th peak of the Himalayas, in Asia, 25,695 feet high, is the loftiest mountain in the world.

SIMPLE FACTS TO PRESERVE HEALTH.

It is remarked during long observation in the hospitals, that the cases of death occurring in rooms averted from the light of the sun, were four times more numerous than the fatal cases in the rooms exposed to the direct action of the solar rays. When poison is swallowed, a good off-hand remedy is to mix salt and mustard, 1 heaped teaspoonful of each, in a glass of water, and drink immediately. It is quick in its operation. Then give the whites of two eggs in a cup of coffee, or the eggs alone if coffee cannot be had: For acid poisons give acids. In cases of opium poisoning, give strong coffee and keep moving. For light burns or scalds, dip the part in cold water or in flour; if the skin is destroyed, cover with varnish. If you fall into the water, float on the back, with the nose and mouth projecting. For apoplexy, raise the head and body; for fainting, lay the person flat. Suck poisoned wounds, unless your mouth is sore. Enlarge the wound, or better cut out the part without delay, cauterize it with caustic, the end of a cigar or a hot coal. If an artery is cut, compress above the wound; if a vein is cut, compress below. If choked, get upon all-fours and cough. Before passing through smoke take a full breath, stoop low, then go ahead; but if you fear carbonic acid gas, walk erect and be careful. Smother a fire with blankets or carpets; water tends to spread burning oil and increase the danger. Remove dust from the eyes by dashing water into them, and avoid rubbing. Remove cinders, etc., with a soft, smooth wooden point. Preserve health and avoid catching cold by regular diet, healthy food and cleanliness. Sir Astley Cooper said :—The best methods to preserve health are temperance, early rising, and sponging the body every morning with cold water, immediately after getting out of bed. Water diluted with 2 per cent. of carbolic acid will disinfect any room or building, if liberally used as a sprinkle. Diphtheria can be cured by a gargle of lemon juice, swallowing a little so as to reach all the affected parts. To avert cold from the feet, wear two pairs of stockings made from different fabrics, one pair of cotton or silk, the other of wool, and the natural heat of the feet will be preserved if the feet are kept clean. In arranging sleeping rooms the soundest and most refreshing slumber will be enjoyed when the head is towards the north. Late hours and anxious pursuits exhaust vitality, producing disease and premature death, therefore the hours of labor and study should be short. Take abundant exercise and recreation. Be moderate in eating and drinking, using simple and plain diet, avoiding strong drink, tobacco, snuff, opium and every excess. Keep the body warm, the temper calm, serene and placid; shun idleness; if your hands cannot be usefully employed, attend to the cultivation of your minds. For pure health giving fresh air, go to the country. Dr. Stockton Hough asserts that if all the inhabitants of the world were living in cities of the magnitude of London, the human race would become extinct in a century or two. The mean average of human life in the United States is 39½ years, while in New York and Philadelphia it is only 23 years; about 50 per cent. of the deaths in these cities being of children under five years of age. A great percentage of this excessive mortality is caused by bad air and bad food.

REMEDY FOR HEADACHE.—A Parisian physician has published a new remedy for headaches. He uses a mixture of ice and salt, in proportion of one to one-half, as a cold mixture, and this he applies by means of a little purse of silk gauze, with a rim of gutta percha, to limited spots on the head, when rheumatic headaches are felt. It gives instantaneous relief. The application is from ½ minute to 1½ minutes, and the skin is rendered white and hard by the applications.

To Cure a Cold.—Before retiring soak the feet in mustard water as hot as can be endured, the feet should at first be plunged in a pail half full of lukewarm water, adding by degrees very hot water until the desired heat is attained, protecting the body and knees with blankets so to direct the vapor from the water as to induce a good sweat. Next, to two tablespoonfuls of boiling water, add one tablespoonful of white sugar and fourteen drops of strong spirits of camphor. Drink the whole and cuddle in bed under plenty of bed clothes and sleep it off.

Worm Lozenges.—Powdered lump sugar, 10 oz. ; starch, 5 oz. ; mix with mucilage, and to every ounce add 12 grains calomel ; divide in 20 grain lozenges. Dose, two to six.

Cure for Drunkenness.—*Warranted a certain Remedy.* Confine the patient to his room, furnish him with his favorite liquor of discretion, diluted with ¾ of water, as much wine, beer, coffee and tea as he desires, but containing ¼ of spirit ; all the food—the bread, meat and vegetables steeped in spirit and water. On the fifth day of this treatment he has an extreme disgust for spirit, being continually drunk. Keep up this treatment till he no longer desires to eat or drink, and the cure is certain.

Spasms.—Acetate of morphia, 1 gr. ; spirit sal volatile, 1 oz. ; sulphuric ether, 1 oz. ; camphor julep, 4 ozs. Mix. Dose, 1 teaspoonful in a glass of cold water or wine, as required. Keep closely corked and shake well before using.

Ayer's Sarsaparilla.—Take 3 fluid ozs. each of alcohol, fluid extracts of sarsaparilla and of stillingia ; 2 fluid ozs. each extract of yellow-dock and of podophyllin ; 1 oz. sugar; 90 grs. iodide of potassium, and 10 grs. iodide of iron.

Brown's Bronchial Troches.—Take 1 lb. of pulverized extract of licorice ; 1½ lbs. of pulverized sugar ; 4 ozs. of pulverized cubebs ; 4 ozs. pulverized gum arabic ; 1 oz. of pulverized extract conium. Mix.

Filling for Decayed Teeth.—Gutta-percha, softened by heat, is recommended. Dr. Rollfs advises melting a piece of caoutchouc at the end of a wire, and introduce it while warm.

To Extract Teeth with Little or No Pain.—Tincture of aconite, chloroform and alcohol, of each 1 oz. : mix ; moisten two pledgets of cotton with the liquid, and apply to the gums on each side of the tooth to be extracted, holding them in their place with pliers or other instruments for from five to ten minutes, rubbing the gum freely inside and out.

Tooth Wash—To Remove Blackness.—Pure muriatic acid, 1 oz. ; water, 1 oz. ; honey, 2 oz. ; mix. Take a tooth-brush and wet it freely with this preparation, and briskly rub the black teeth, and in a moment's time they will be perfectly white ; then immediately wash out the mouth with water, that the acid may not act upon the *enamel* of the teeth.

Cure for Lock Jaw, said to be Positive—Let any one who has an attack of lock jaw take a small quantity of spirits of turpentine, warm it and pour it on the wound—no matter where the wound is, or what its nature is—and relief will follow in less than one minute. Turpentine is also a sovereign remedy for croup. Saturate a piece of flannel with it, and place the flannel on the throat and chest—and in very severe cases, three to five drops on a lump of sugar may be taken internally.

NAME.	BORN.	DIED.	NAME.	BORN.	DIED.
Abbott, Jacob	1803	1879	Boudinot, Elias	1749	1821
Abbott, John S. C	1805	1877	Boyd, Linn	1800	1859
Abd-el-Kader	1807	1873	Brackenridge, H. M.	1786	1871
About, Edmond	1828	......	Bragg, Braxton	1817	1876
Adams, Charles F	1807	......	Breckenridge, J. C.	1821	1875
Adams, William T	1822	......	Broderick, David C.	1818	1859
Aguilar, Grace	1816	1847	Bronte, Charlotte	1816	1855
Airy, George B	1801	......	Brougham, H., Lord	1779	1868
Albert, Prince	1819	1861	Brown, John	1800	1859
Albert, Edward	1841	......	Browne, Charles F.	1834	1867
Aldrich, T. Bailey	1836	......	Browning, Eliz. B.	1809	1861
Alexander I. of Russia	1777	1825	Browning, Orville H.	1810	1881
Alexander II	1818	1881	Brownlow, Wm. G.	1805	1877
Alison, Sir Archibald.	1792	1867	Brownson, Orestes A	1803	1876
Allston, Washington.	1779	1843	Buchanan, James	1791	1868
Andersen, Hans C	1805	1875	Buckle, Henry Thos.	1822	1862
Anderson, Robert	1805	1871	Bulwer, Lytton, Lord	1805	1873
Andrew, John A	1818	1867	Bunsen, C. J. K.,		
Antonelli, Giacomo	1806	1877	Baron	1791	1868
Armstrong, John	1755	1843	Burnside, Amb. E.	1824	1881
Arnold, Benedict	1740	1801	Butler, Benj. F., of		
Arnold, Thomas	1795	1842	N. Y	1795	1858
Asbury, Francis	1745	1816	Byron, G. N. G., Lord	1788	1824
Astor, John Jacob	1763	1848	Calhoun, John C	1782	1850
Austen, Jane	1775	1817	Campbell, Alex.	1788	1866
Bache, Alex. Dallas.	1806	1867	Campbell, John A	1811	......
Baillie, Joanna	1762	1851	Campbell, Thomas.	1777	1844
Bainbridge, Wm	1774	1833	Canning, George	1770	1827
Balfe, Michael Wm	1808	1870	Carey, Henry C	1793	1879
Bancroft, George	1800	......	Carlyle, Thomas	1795	1881
Barlow, Francis C	1834	......	Carroll, Charles	1737	1832
Beauregard, P. G. T.	1818	......	Cavour, Camillo	1810	1861
Beecher, Henry W	1813	......	Chalmers, Thomas	1780	1847
Beecher, Lyman	1775	1863	Channing, Wm. E.	1780	1842
Beethoven, Ludwig.	1770	1827	Chantrey, Sir F	1781	1841
Bell, John	1797	1869	Chase, Salmon P.	1808	1873
Bellini, Vincenzio.	1802	1835	Chopin, F	1810	1849
Bennett, J. Gordon	1795	1872	Clarke, Adam	1760	1832
Béranger, P. J. de	1780	1857	Clarkson, Thomas	1760	1846
Binney, Horace	1780	1875	Clay, Cassius M	1810	......
Bismarck, Prince von	1815	......	Clay, Henry	1777	1852
Blair, Francis P	1791	1877	Clayton, John M	1796	1856
Bolivar, Simon	1783	1830	Clemens, Samuel L.	1835	......
Bonaparte, Jerome	1784	1860	Clinton, De Witt	1769	1828
Bonaparte, Louis	1778	1846	Cobbett, William	1762	1835
Bonaparte, Lucien	1775	1840	Cobden, Richard	1804	1865
Bonaparte, Napoleon	1769	1821	Colburn, Warren	1793	1833
Booth, Junius B	1796	1852	Cole, Thomas	1801	1848
			Coleridge, Samuel T.	1772	1834

NAME.	BORN.	DIED.
Collins, Wm. Wilkie	1825	......
Cooper, Sir Astley	1768	1841
Cooper, J. Fenimore	1789	1851
Cornwallis, Charles	1738	1805
Corwin, Thomas	1794	1865
Cowper, William	1731	1800
Crabbe, George	1754	1832
Crawford, Thomas	1814	1857
Croker, John Wilson	1780	1857
Cruikshank, George	1792	1878
Curran, John Philpot	1750	1817
Curtis, Benjamin R	1809	1874
Curtis, George Wm	1824	......
Cushing, Caleb	1800	1879
Cushman, Charlotte	1816	1876
Custer, George A	1839	1876
Cuvier, G. C. L. D., Bar	1769	1832
Dallas, Alexander J	1759	1817
Dallas, George M	1792	1864
Dana, James D	1813	......
Dana, Richard H	1787	1879
Dana, Richard H., Jr.	1815	1882
Darwin, Charles R	1809	1882
Davenport, Edw. L	1816	1877
Davis, Charles H	1807	1877
Davis, David	1815	......
Davis, Jefferson	1808	......
Davy, Sir Humphrey	1778	1829
Dearborn, Henry	1751	1821
Decatur, Stephen	1779	1820
Dalaroche, Paul	1797	1856
De Quincey, Thomas	1785	1859
Derby, Edw., Earl	1799	1869
Dickens, Charles	1812	1870
Dickinson, John	1732	1808
Disraeli, Benjamin	1805	1881
Disraeli, Isaac	1776?	1848
Dix, John A	1798	1879
Dixon, W. Hepworth	1821	1879
Donizetti, Gaetano	1798	1848
Doré, Paul Gustave	1833	......
Duane, William J	1780	1865
Du Chaillu, Paul B	1830	......
Dudevant (George Sand)	1804	1876
Dumas, Alexandre	1803	1870
Dwight, Timothy	1752	1817
Early, Jubel A	1818	......
Eastlake, Sir Chas. L	1793	1865
Eaton, John Henry	1790	1856
Edgeworth, Maria	1767	1849
Elliot, Ebenezer	1781	1849
Elliot, Jesse D	1782	1845
Emerson, Ralph Waldo	1803	1882
Emmet, Robert	1780	1803
Ericsson, John	1803	......
Erskine, Thos., Lord	1750	1823
Evarts, William M	1818	......
Everett, Edward	1794	1865
Ewing, Thomas	1789	1871
Farragut, David G	1801	1870
Field, Cyrus W	1819	......
Field, David Dudley	1805	......
Field, Stephen J	1816	......
Fillmore, Millard	1800	1874
Fish, Hamilton	1808	......
Floyd, John B	1805	1863
Forrest, Edwin	1806	1872
Forsyth, John	1780	1841
Fox, Charles James	1749	1806
Franklin, Sir John	1786	1847
Froude, James Anthony	1818	......
Fulton, Robert	1765	1815
Gambetta, Leon	1838	......
Garfield, James A	1831	1881
Garibaldi, Giuseppe	1807	1882
Garrison, W. Lloyd	1804	1879
Gaskell, Eliz. C	1811	1865
Gautier, Theophile	1811	1872
George III	1738	1820
George IV	1762	1830
Gibson, John	1790	1866
Giles, Wm. Branch	1762	1830
Gillmore, Quincey A	1825	......
Girard, Stephen	1750	1831
Gladstone, Wm. E	1809	......
Goethe, J. W. von	1749	1832
Goodrich, Sam. G	1793	1860
Goodyear, Charles	1800	1860
Gough, John B	1817	......
Gounod, Felix C	1818	......
Grant, Ulysses S	1822	......
Grattan, Henry	1746	1820
Gray, Asa	1810	......
Greeley, Horace	1811	1872
Grier, Robert C	1794	1876
Grimm, Jacob L. C	1785	1863
Griswold, Rufus W	1815	1857
Grote, George	1794	1871
Guizot, F. P. G	1787	1874
Gurney, Joseph J	1788	1847
Guthrie, James	1792	1869
Haeckel, Ernst H	1834	......
Hale, John P	1806	1873
Halevy, Jacques	1799	1862
Haliburton, T. C	1797	1865
Hall, Robert	1764	1831
Hallam, Henry	1777	1859
Hamilton, Sir Wm	1788	1856
Hamlin, Hannibal	1809	......
Hancock, Winfield S.	1824	......
Harrison, Wm. Henry	1773	1841
Hastings, Warren	1733	1818

NAME.	BORN.	DIED.	
Mifflin, Thomas	1744	1800	Pier
Mill, John Stuart	1806	1873	Pier
Miller, Hugh	1802	1856	Pier
Miller, Samuel F.	1816	......	Pinl
Milne-Edwards, H.	1800	......	Pitt,
Mitchell, Donald G.	1822	......	Pius
Moltke, H. C. B. von	1800	......	Poe,
Montalembert, Comte			Polk
de.	1810	1870	Pors
Montgomery, James	1771	1854	Port
Moore, Thomas	1779	1852	Port
More, Hannah	1745	1833	Pow
Moreau, J. Victor	1763	1813	Pres
Morgan, Daniel	1736	1802	Pres
Morgan, S. O. Lady	1783	1859	Prie
Morse, Jedediah	1761	1826	Proc
Morse, Samuel F. V.	1791	1872	Pug
Morton, Oliver P.	1823	1877	Quil
Motley, John L.	1814	1877	Rac
Müller, F. Max	1823	......	Ran
Murat, Joachim	1771	1815	Rea
Murchison, Sir R.	1792	1871	Rec
Murray, Lindley	1745	1826	A.
Napoleon I	1769	1821	Reli
Napoleon II	1811	1832	Rica
Napoleon III	1808	1873	Riel
Nast, Thomas	1840	......	Rine
Nelson, Horatio	1758	1805	Rist
Nelson, Samuel	1792	1873	Roch
Newman, Francis W.	1805	......	, de
Newman, John H.	1801	......	Rog
Ney, Michel	1769	1815	Ron
Nicholas I	1796	1855	Ross
O'Connell, Daniel	1775	1847	Ross
Offenbach, Jacques	1819	1880	Rus
Ossoli, Margaret Ful-			Rus
ler.	1810	1850	Rus
Owen, Robert	1771	1858	Rus
Owen, Robert Dale	1801	1877	Ruth
Paganini, Niccolo	1784	1840	Sant
Page, William	1811	......	L
Paley, William	1743	1805	Sarg
Palmerston, Lord	1784	1865	Schi
Park, Mungo	1771	1805	Sch
Parker, Theodore	1810	1860	Schu
Parton, James	1822	......	Schu
Parton, Sara Payson	1811	1872	Scot
Patti, Adelina	1843	......	Scri
Patti, Charlotta	1840	......	Sedg
Paulding, James K.	1779	1860	Serg
Peabody, George	1795	1869	Sew
Pedro II., of Brazil	1825	......	Seyi
Peel, Sir Robert	1788	1850	She
Peirce, Benjamin	1809	1880	She
Pellico, Silvio	1789	1854	She
Percival, James G.	1795	1857	She
Phillips, Wendell	1811	......	She
Pickering, Timothy	1745	1829	She

NAME.	BORN.	DIED.	NAME.	BORN.	DIED.
Sherman, William T.	1820	......	Tupper, Martin F.	1810	......
Shields, James.	1810	1879	Turner, J. M. W.	1775	1851
Siddons, Sarah.	1755	1831	Twiggs, David E.	1790	1862
Siliman, Benjamin.	1779	1864	Tyler, John.	1790	1862
Simms, Wm. Gilmore.	1806	1870	Uhland, Johann L.	1787	1862
Simon, Jules.	1814	......	Upshur, Abel P.	1790	1844
Smith, Gerrit.	1797	1874	Ure, Andrew.	1778	1857
Smith, Joseph.	1805	1844	Vallandigham, C. L.	1822	1871
Slidell, John.	1793	1871	Van Buren, Martin.	1782	1862
Smith, Sidney.	1771	1845	Vanderbilt, C.	1794	1877
Smithson, Jas. L. M.	1765	1829	Verdi, Giuseppe.	1814	......
Somerville, Mary.	1780	1872	Vernet, Horace.	1789	1863
Soult, Nicholas Jean.	1769 ?	1851	Victor Emmanuel II.	1820	1878
Southey, Robert.	1774	1843	Victoria, Alexandrina	1819	......
Sparks, Jared.	1789	1866	Villemain, Abel F.	1790	1867
Spencer, John C.	1788	1855	Wade, Benjamin F.	1800	1878
Stanhope, P. H., Earl	1805	1875	Wagner, Richard.	1813	......
Stanton, Edwin M.	1814	1869	Waite, Morrison R.	1816	......
Stephens, Alex. H.	1812	......	Walker, Robert J.	1801	1869
Stevens, Thaddeus.	1793	1868	Washburne, Elihu B.	1816	......
Stevenson, Andrew.	1784	1857	Watt, James.	1736	1819
Stewart, Charles.	1778	1869	Wayne, James M.	1790	1867
Stockton, Robert F.	1796	1866	Weber, Karl M. von.	1786	1826
Stoddert, Benjamin.	1751	1813	Webster, Noah.	1758	1843
Story, Joseph.	1779	1845	Welles, Gideon.	1802	1878
Stowe, Harriet B.	1812	......	Wellington, Duke of	1769	1852
Stuart, Alex. H. H.	1807	......	West, Benjamin.	1738	1820
Stuart, Gilbert.	1755	1828	Whatley, Richard.	1787	1863
Stuart, James E. B.	1832	1864	Wheaton, Henry.	1785	1848
Sue, Eugène.	1804	1857	Wheeler, William A.	1819	......
Sullivan, James.	1744	1808	Whewell, William.	1794	1863
Sully, Thomas.	1783	1872	Whitney, Eli.	1765	1825
Sumner, Charles.	1811	1874	Whittier, John G.	1807	......
Taglioni, Marie.	1804	......	Wickliffe, Charles A.	1788	1869
Talfourd, T. N.	1794	1854	Wieland, C. M.	1733	1813
Talleyrand-Perigord.	1754	1838	Wilberforce, Wm.	1759	1833
Talma, Francois Jos.	1763	1826	Wilkes, Charles.	1801	1877
Taney, Roger B.	1777	1864	Wilkie, Sir David.	1785	1841
Taylor, Bayard.	1825	1878	Wilkinson, James.	1757	1825
Taylor, Isaac.	1613 ?	1865	William IV.	1765	1837
Taylor, Zachary.	1784	1850	Wilmot, David.	1814	1868
Tegner, Esaias.	1782	1846	Wilson, Alexander.	1766	1813
Tennyson, Alfred.	1809 ?	......	Wilson, Henry.	1812	1875
Thackeray, W. M.	1811	1863	Wilson, John.	1785	1854
Thierry, J. N. A.	1795	1856	Winthrop, Robert C.	1809	......
Thiers, Louis Adolphe	1797	1877	Wirt, William.	1772	1834
Thomas, George H.	1816	1870	Wise, Henry A.	1806	1876
Thorwaldsen, Bertel.	1770	1844	Wiseman, Cardinal.	1822	1865
Tieck, Ludwig.	1773	1853	Wolcott, Oliver.	1760	1833
Tilden, Samuel J.	1814	......	Woodbury, Levi.	1789	1851
Tompkins, Daniel B.	1774	1825	Woodworth, Samuel.	1785	1842
Tooke, J. Horne.	1736	1812	Wool, John E.	1784	1869
Toombs, Robert.	1810	......	Worcester, Joseph E.	1784	1865
Trumbull, John.	1756	1843	Wordsworth, Wm.	1770	1850
Trumbull, Jonathan.	1740	1809	Wraxall, Sir N. W.	1751	1831
Truxton, Thomas.	1755	1822	Wright, Silas.	1795	1847
Tucker, St. George.	1752	1827	Wythe, George.	1726	1806
Tuckerman, H. T.	1813	1871	Young, Brigham.	1801	1877

DICTIONARY OF MUSICAL TERMS.

Accompaniment. A secondary part added to the principal for the improvement of the general effect.
Adagio. A slow movement.
Ad libitum. Implies that the time of the movement is left to the discretion of the performer.
Allegretto. With cheerful quickness.
Andante. Somewhat sedate ; slowly.
A temp. In regular time.
Beat. An indication of a certain duration of time.
Calando. A gradual diminution in speed and tone.
Chromatic. Proceeding or formed by semi-tones.
Con. With ; as Con expressione. *Cresendo.* A gradual increase in tone.
Da. By. *Delicato.* With delicacy.
Dales, or *Dal.* In a soft, quiet manner.
Doloroso. In a melancholy, sad style.
Expressiov, or *Con cæpressione.* With expression.
Fine. The end. *Fork,* or *For.* Strong, loud.
Furioso. With great animation. *Giusto.* In perfect time.
Grave. The slowest time or movement.
Gusto, Con gusto. With style ; taste. *Il.* The.
Impetuoso. Impetuously. *In.* In ; as In tempo.
Intrado, or *Introduzione.* An introduction to a piece of music.
Largo. A slow and solemn degree of time.
Legato. In a smooth, even manner. *Leggiando.* Lightly.
Marcato. In a marked manner. *Meme.* The same.
Moderato. Moderately. *Malto.* Very ; as Malto forte.
Obligato. An essential portion of a composition.
Ottava, or *8va.* An octave.
Pedale, or *Ped.* Signifies that performer must press down pedal.
Pen. A little. *Piano,* or *P.* Soft.
Pianissimo, or *PP.* Very soft. *Plus.* More.
Poco a poco. Gradually ; by a regular gradation.
Premiere. First ; as Premiere fois ; first time.
Presto. Very quick. *Primo.* As Violino primo, first violin.
Quasi. In the manner of ; like. *Quieto.* With repose, quietly.
Ritenente, Ritenuto. Decreasing in speed.
Segno. Sign ; as al segno, go back to sign.
Solo, Sola. Alone. A composition rendered by one person.
Sostenuto, or *Sost.* Prolonged ; sustained. *Spirito.* With spirit.
Staccato. Each note to be distinctly marked. *Stesso.* The same.
Syncopation. Connecting the last note of a bar with the first note of the following, thus forming one prolonged with a duration equal to the two.
Tardo. Slowly. *Tempo Comodo.* Conveniently.
Theme. A subject. *Tranquillo.* Tranquilly.
Tremendi. With terrific expression.
Trille, or *Trillo.* A trill or shake.
Trio. A composition for three performers.
Triplet. A group of three notes equal in duration of time to two notes of the same value.
Un A. As un poco, a little. *Veloce.* Rapidly.

THE DAYS OF THE WEEK AND THE MONTHS OF THE YEAR.

DAYS OF THE WEEK.

SUNDAY, the first day of the week, was originally so called because it was specially devoted to the worship of the sun, regarded as the first and greatest of pagan deities. As associated with Christianity, it is more correct to call it the Lord's Day, Jesus having risen on the first day of the week.

MONDAY, the second day of the week, is so called because it was dedicated by ancient pagans, and especially by the early Saxons, to the worship of the moon.

TUESDAY, the third day of the week, was dedicated by the ancient Saxons to the worship of Tuisco, the god of war.

WEDNESDAY, the fourth day of the week, was observed by the ancient Saxons in honor of Woden.—*Ash Wednesday*, the first day of Lent, so called from the Roman Catholic practice of sprinkling ashes on the head in token of penitence.

THURSDAY, the fifth day of the week, was observed by the ancient Saxons on account of Thor, supposed to be a deity of the Scandinavians.

FRIDAY, the sixth day of the week, so called from Frea, or Friga, a Saxon goddess. On account of the Crucifixion occurring on the sixth day of the week, it is observed by the Church of England and the Church of Rome as a fast.

SATURDAY, the seventh day of the week, so called from Seater, a Saxon deity corresponding to Saturn. Saturday is still universally observed as the Sabbath by Jews.

THE MONTHS.

The twelve months of the modern year are called calendar months, to distinguish them from lunar months, of which there are thirteen and a fraction of a fourteenth annually. The calendar is a list of all the days of the year.

JANUARY. Its name is said by some to be derived from Janus, a Roman deity, who was supposed to preside over the new year as well as over all new undertakings. But others say that it was derived from *anua*, a gate.

FEBRUARY, derives its name from *Februa*, a feast held by the Romans on the 15th of the month in honor of Lupercus, the god of fertility. February having usually twenty-eight days, but twenty-nine days every fourth year, each such year is called therefore bissextile, or leap year, distinguished by being equally divisible by four.

MARCH, the third month of the year, was not so regarded until 1751. It was regarded as the first month by Romulus, the supposed son of Mars, the god of war, whence the name of the month was derived.

APRIL, the fourth month of the year, so called from *aperilis*, I open, the month of the opening of buds and fertility.

MAY, the fifth month of the year, the name being derived from Maia, the mother of Mercury, to whom the first of the month was dedicated as a festival, thus originating May Day.

JUNE, the sixth month of the year, is supposed to have derived its name from Junius Brutus.

JULY, the seventh month of the year, so called in honor of Julius Cæsar, who adjusted the old Roman calendar upon its present plan, B. C. 46.

AUGUST, the eighth month of the year, derives its name from Augustus Cæsar.

SEPTEMBER, the ninth month of the year, still retains its original Roman name, derived from *septem*, seven, it having been the seventh month of the calendar of Romulus.

OCTOBER, the tenth month of the year, like the previous one, retains its old Roman name, derived from *octo*, eight, in which order it was placed under Romulus.

NOVEMBER, the eleventh month of the year, but the ninth of the early Roman period, hence called from *novem*, nine.

DECEMBER, the twelfth month of the year, but the tenth of the old Roman calendar, hence called from *decem*, ten. Being the reverse month of June, the shortest day of the year is always the 21st.

FLAVORING EXTRACTS.

O UR EXTRACTS *are made only from the Finest Vanilla Bean and Choicest Fruits, of natural color and flavor. Absolutely Pure, only one quality—Extra Fine—strictly adhered to. Put up in packages easily recognized, original and unique. Their Excellence and Purity will commend their extensive use, by a discriminating public.*

J. E. BURNS & CO.,
PHILADELPHIA.

DISINFECT YOUR HOMES WITH

AROMATIC THYMOLA

DIFFUSED BY

THE BRACKET HOLDER AND EVAPORATOR.

A POWERFUL, WHOLESOME PURIFIER.

Prevents

CHOLERA,
DIPHTHERIA,
MALARIA,
SCARLET FEVER,
TYPHOID FEVER,
AND ALL
INFECTIOUS
DISEASES.

Corrects

BAD ODORS
AND
DELETERIOUS
GASES.

An Effective

Ærial antiseptic. Corrects zymotic influences. It is a neat article, and so arranged that more or less of the element can be diffused at will.

Exceeds

All other elements for disinfecting and deodorizing infected air. Is very pleasant and invigorating in the sick room. Every family should have it.

For Use in

BED ROOMS,
NURSERIES,
CLOSETS,
RAILWAY CARS,
KITCHENS,
STATE ROOMS,
OFFICES,
COTTAGES,
SCHOOLS,
HOSPITAL
WARDS,
Etc., Etc.

For Mosquitoes.

The very many features this little Bracket has to recommend it cannot all be explained here, or could you fully comprehend it without seeing it; it costs but a trifle. We can find a remedy for almost all inconveniences at the seashore except MOSQUITOES. You can enjoy LIFE even in that respect if you wish, because other things have failed, do not condemn this without a trial, it is worth all it costs, which is a small amount for the comfort it insures.

Ask for

Aromatic Thymola diffused by the bracket-Holder and Evaporator.

PRICE, 50 CENTS.

J. H. BLAKE & CO., Chemists,

Laboratory, 425 Locust Street,

Sole Manufacturers. ——— PHILADELPHIA, PA.

FOR SALE BY ALL DRUGGISTS.

.

www.ingramcontent.com/pod-product-compliance
Lightning Source LLC
Chambersburg PA
CBHW020027030726
47499CB00007B/2301